Flip Side of the Game:

Triple Crown Collection

Flip Side of the Game:

Triple Crown Collection

Tu-Shonda L. Whitaker

www.urbanbooks.net

Urban Books, LLC
97 N18th Street
Wyandanch, NY 11798

Flip Side of the Game: Triple Crown Collection
Copyright © 2004 Triple Crown Publications LLC

This title is published by Urban Books, LLC under a
licensing agreement with Triple Crown Publications
LLC.

ISBN 13: 978-1-62286-992-3
ISBN 10: 1-62286-992-3

First Mass Market Printing May 2016
First Trade Paperback Printing (July 2004)
Printed in the United States of America

10 9 8 7 6 5 4 3 2 1

*This is a work of fiction. Any references or similarities
to actual events, real people, living or dead, or to
real locales are intended to give the novel a sense of
reality. Any similarity in other names, characters,
places, and incidents is entirely coincidental.*

Distributed by Kensington Publishing Corp.
Submit Orders to:
Customer Service
400 Hahn Road
Westminster, MD 21157-4627
Phone: 1-800-733-3000
Fax: 1-800-659-2436

Dedications

To my parents, my husband, and my children. Moreover, in loving memory of my grandparents, Lucy and Sip Whitaker; my grandfather, Phillip Parker; my Aunt Tom; and my godmother, Leola Atkinson. You are truly, truly missed.

Acknowledgments

No word is spoken, and no word is written without Hallelujahs! Be it to the glory of the coming of the Lord, for without God and His son Jesus Christ, there would be no spirit, no talent, and no storytelling in my soul. So, there is no looking back, because everything, by the grace of God and in the name of Jesus Christ, lies ahead.

My mother, Barbara Whitaker, and my father, Melvin Parker, what would I do without you? You have been everything to me, and nobody in the world could have greater parents than you! You are the epitome of love and strength, and for that, I thank you!

My two li'l divas, Taylor and Sydney, as God has blessed me to be in your life and bring you into this world, I can only hope and pray that I stand up to be the mother that He requires of me. I thank you for allowing me to be a mommy and a writer at the same time. It's a tough job, but somebody's gotta do it! Mommy loves you more than anything! I hope and pray to teach you that you have the ability to do anything that you set your mind to.

My husband, Kevin Lake, thanks for listening to me read a line here and a line there. Thanks for all the belief, love, support, and a triple thanks for being the best living room editor that anyone can ever, ever, ever, have. P.S.: Much respect to the Trini masses. "Trini to the bone!"

To my grandmother, Lizzie Parker, thanks for being who you are. Don't ever change.

All homage and respect given to my ancestors, from whose loins my family and I have come.

To the six oldest women in my family: Lizzie Parker, Iruth Williams, Elsie Askew, Eunice Stephenson, O'dessa Askew, and Vivian Bush. There is strength and honor in you that God has blessed me to be part of. Your lives and your stories are filled with a richness that words cannot speak and a written story could never map. May God always bless you, and may I grow to be as graceful as you all are.

To Aunt Phyllis, thanks for the encouragement and belief. Who could have a bigger fan of literature than you?

To Aunt Deborah and my uncle, Minister Millard Hardaway, thanks for the constant encouragement. May God bless you as you travel the road to continued and renewed strength in Him.

To Uncle Sip and Aunt Gerri, my children's godparents, Renee and Kevin, Phine and Ricky, thanks for all the all the love and support.

To my aunts and uncles, Sharon, Yolanda, Lonnie-Lee, James (J.D.), and Donald, and to my family in and around my homctown of Murfreesboro, North Carolina, the Robinsons and the Parkers, thanks for your love and support. To my cousin, Antwain "Mark," you know what's up. Do the right thing, 'cause you got it like that.

To Aunt Geraldine Boone in Norfolk, Virginia, thanks for the e-mails! And thanks to my family in Norfolk, the Greens and the Boones.

To my family in Jersey City, the Askews and Johnsons, you all are always there to offer your love and support in everything that I do, and for that, I say thank you.

To my cousins, John, Kaareem (my children's godfather), Taniesha, Malik, and Sharief, damn, who knew the li'l kids from Newark would grow up and one of them would have written a book! God is good!

To my cousins, Gerard, Jaquan, Kristen, Korynn, RaShea, Rayanna, Kenya-Amir, Tiana, Nia, Aashir, Isaiah, TeAunda, and Marquise, as you grow and become beautiful black men and women, I hope and pray that you stop along the way to enjoy your childhood; that you leave adult things and adult situations for when you are adults; that you know that education is no joke! Go to school, learn, and be true to yourself.

To my aunts, Mae and Carol, and to my extended families, the Smiths, the Simmons, and my Trinidadian Lake and Bailey in-laws, thanks for the love and support, and to my cousin Monique, who said, "Shonda, you wrote a book? Oh my God, my li'l cousin done grew up!"

To my *sistafied* girlfriends, Valerie, Sharonda, Lisa S.H., Lisa G.W., and Lisa P., I thank you for your friendship. I can only hope and pray that as we grow and become more prominent African American women, we continue to move in such a way that pays homage to our ancestors, and that we always remember from where and which we have come. In the famous words of Valerie Hall, "That's wassup!" Oh, and Lisa (Scofield), thanks for receiving and reviewing all the faxes and all of the phone calls, where I said, "Lisa, how does this sound?" Girlfriend, you know I'll never forget the Alizé and the book club meeting.

To Lisa Gibson-Wilson, who said, "Gurrrrl, I am feelin' this one!" I must say thank you, as I can only imagine that if I had a big sister, she and her husband would give me some of the same advice that you and Julian have shared. Always be blessed!

To Uncle Donald, there is but one God, and He is in the biggest business of blessing us with second chances. Please be strong and hold on. Something will happen for you, and prayerfully you will be home with us soon.

Larry Karpati, to simply say thank you would be a major understatement for all of the encouragement that you have given me! This one's for you, baby!

To my godsons, Micah and Christopher, God-mommy loves you!

To Pastor Edward A. Allen and the congregation of Philemon Missionary Baptist Church, thanks for your love and support.

Thanks to Renaissance Management Services!

To Vickie Stringer, for a chance, *Let That Be the Reason* that I say thank you!

To the entire Triple Crown family, thanks for welcoming me to Triple Crown, and may we each reach the height of literary success!

To Kathleen Jackson, thank you, thank you, thank you! Trust and believe, you have it going on, girlfriend. In the beginning, *Flip Side of the Game* started out with an editor, but in the end, I gained a friend. Keep in touch, and the sequel to *Flip Side of the Game* is on its way!

Special shout outs to Arena Sports Bar in Brick City, the best artist in the world, Malik Whitaker of www.m-printarts.com, Easy Connect Cell Phone store on Bloomfield Avenue in Newark, and Ahmadi's Hair Creation in Union, New Jersey.

I must thank my own; my mother's, my aunts' and uncles' friends, coworkers, and book club members; the book stores; distributors; S.W.A.P.; my college professor Dr. Margot Banks; my second grade teacher Wanda Bishop; Deborah Smith (thanks for falling in love with the character Aunt Cookie!); my godmother Joyce Moore (continue to spread your love to all the children that you take into your home); Ms. Mary (thanks for braiding Sydney's hair and loving her like she was your own); and a special thanks to the best financial advisor in Harlem, Julian Wilson.

And to all of those whom I love dearly, but may have inadvertently not mentioned, please do not hold it against me, charge it to my head and not my heart, for I appreciate all of you and all of the parts that you have played in my life.

As always, saving the best for last, to all of my readers, thanks for your support! I would love to know what you think of my first novel, *Flip Side of the Game*. Please e-mail me at info@tushonda.com and be sure to look out for the upcoming Web site.

One love and many blessings,
Tu-Shonda

The Ground Floor

Life is a mu'fucka, and that's the God honest truth. I have been grown all of my life, and that has worked to my benefit, I believe.

When I first greeted the scene, I arrived in a black plastic bag, found in a trash dump, addicted to crack with a note that read: *Please forgive me. My mother's only fifteen.* Well, that shit musta been a joke, because the trick that calls herself my mother, also known as Rowanda Wright, is a chickenhead that I want no parts of.

The State of New York raised me, for the most part. Rowanda Wright was fifteen when she had me, addicted to crack, and living on the streets. My grandmother was in an eighteen-month rehab and had just graduated the program when she heard that Rowanda had been arrested for putting me in a Hefty CinchSak. After that, social services gave me to my rehabilitated grandmother, which was a dressed-up word for a functioning methadone queen.

We never had any furniture, food, money, or any time to be children. There were three of us who were born grown, and no, we didn't come from the same pussy. Rowanda had a twin, Towanda, and they were both cracked the fuck out. My grandmother tried, but she could never kick the habit, and when methadone didn't work, she shot up dope and mixed the shit with coke.

And Daddy? Humph, who he?

Lincoln Street Projects was all that I had ever known for the first eight years of my life, and what I discovered was that the projects had moments when it was in a groove of silence—a time when it could mix the tranquility of night with the drumbeat of the piss-filled hallways, and the high-pitched clapping of the steel doors against metal frames. It was a quiet noise, where you could hear clearly how Ms. Johnson got her ass kicked every night, how the two girls next door were more than just friends, and how Grandma was in the bathroom tappin' on the wrong vein, falling down, and slamming her head against the cold iron of the lion-claw tub.

Rowanda found Grandma naked and bleeding, with her body stretched out like Jesus on the crucifix, a hypodermic needle in the cradle of her vagina, and blood running like calm waters down the side of her face, rippling over her breast.

Grandma's man took off and ran, with the lingering clink of his belt buckle dragging behind him. His splash in the puddle of Grandma's blood held his footprints as he made his way out, with his pants in one hand and the rest of his and Grandma's stash in the other.

Sirens ringing, church folks singing, and half the congregation was getting high. The social worker came to give me a speech about having a home and a new type of peace. All I could do was obey, 'cause not even my mother knew where I was gonna stay. And relatives? Puh-leeze! Most of them either had their own social services cases, were in prison, dopefiends, or plain out didn't give a fuck.

The day that Grandma went to Heaven's ghetto, I stayed in the social services office all day and half of the night. Then a lady came in with a low haircut dyed bleached blonde and crème-de-café skin. She wore magenta lipstick, tight Levi jeans, with red high heels, and a midriff black tank top. She smacked her lips when she spoke, and the first thing she said was, "Rowanda Wright sent me here."

"And you are?" the social worker asked.

"Larry Turner's sista."

"Larry Turner?"

"He's my brotha. Vera Wright-Turner, her mama, say she's my niece. I'm Cookie Turner. And you are?"

"The social worker for Vera."

"Mm-hmm. Well, I just found out today that Larry had a chile, so I came to see what her eyes look like, and that'll let me know if she is a Turner for sure. And if so, she ain't never got to worry 'bout the state of New York, 'cause she will have a home with me."

Since I was born grown with an innate ability to hustle, I didn't wait until the social worker came to give me some long speech about this lady, me needing a home, and who Larry Turner was. I ran out of the social worker's office, grabbed this lady by both her legs, and cried into her belly pouch to please take me. She didn't think once about my eyes. She raised my head, kissed the crooked part between my two corn rolls, and said, "Let's go."

When I got there, I suddenly realized that I didn't know this lady, and she damn sure didn't know me. I was scared to death, because I had never seen anyone like her. Her wrists were draped in silver bangles, and her hoop earrings were so big that they rested on her shoulders. It seemed that she had a passion for smoking cigarettes, cussin', and walking around the house with her bra and tight jeans on.

She held one phone conversation after another, laughing and carrying on, all the while smoking cigarettes and listening to Marvin Gaye. I knew instantly that she ain't take no shit, and being that I didn't know her and she didn't know me, I ain't say two words for a week. Hell, what was I going to say? Who are you? Who is Larry Turner? How come, after all these years, somebody say that I got a daddy and you're his sister, but where he at? And how come you ain't gettin' high right in front of me? Why is there always food in your refrigerator? Does that mean that I should stop stealing food out the pantry and hiding it under my bed? And, by the way, anybody seen Rowanda?

So, instead of asking these things, I just watched and became amused. Aunt Cookie had a live-in boyfriend, Boydon Brown, who I called Uncle Boy. It was 1982, and Uncle Boy still wore bell-bottom pants, long sideburns, and a thick mustache. He was caramel-colored, and the way Aunt Cookie looked at him was like he was so fine that she could just taste his sweetness on her tongue. But she didn't take no mess from him either, and he knew better than to bring the noise up in Cookie Turner's row-house, 'cause she didn't play that shit.

Aunt Cookie walked around her living room, crushing orange-speckled industrial carpet under her feet, Marvin Gaye singing the hell outta "Sexual Healing", and check this: she had incense burning, and this chick wasn't even smokin' a spliff! What the fuck was that? This was the first person I had ever met in the eight years of my life who had incense burning just for the hell of it.

I was speechless. I just sat back and waited for the moment when she pulled out a hit, started noddin' off, or when Uncle Boy hauled off and slapped the shit out of her 'cause he felt like it.

"I guess it's just me, you, and Uncle Boy, Babygirl," Aunt Cookie said to me, patting the bottom of her soft pack of Newports in an effort to loosen up a cigarette. She held the phone to her ear, and had just gotten finished telling one of her girlfriends that wasn't nothin' goin' on but the rent.

"This is home, Babygirl," she continued to say, with a cigarette hanging out of her mouth. "Ain't no place else after this."

I just looked around, 'cause I knew this bitch was either rich or she was boostin' mad shit, 'cause she had the flyest place I had ever seen in my life: a plastic-covered crushed velvet living room set, carpet, a tiger floor rug hanging on the wall, and a color television.

"So, what you think?" Aunt Cookie asked, hanging the phone up and then taking a pull from her Newport. "You think you might like living here? All we got is each other."

"I think that all you do is run yo' mouth," I said to Aunt Cookie. "And you need to practice being quiet before Uncle Boy knock the shit out of you. Just some advice. And another thing: Is you boostin' and shit? 'Cause, I done had enough raids in my day to save my mu'fuckin' life. I know that you ain't got this fly shit in yo' crib by magic. The niggas I know ain't just straight-up livin' like this!"

"Come again, Babygirl?" Aunt Cookie asked, taking a long hard pull off her cigarette, blowing out a string of smoke, and then mashing the cigarette into the orange marble ash tray. "Run that pass me again."

"Look, Aunt Cookie," I said, beginning to feel slightly comfortable with my newfound aunt. "Every time I turn around, your mouth is on fire with one cuss after the next, and yo' nigga, he don't even check you or nothin'. That's some real live shit, homegirl. And then, I'm lookin' at you and I ain't seen you nod, scratch, or sniff yet. I mean, really, is you boostin'? Tell me, 'cause I done seen it all." Then I reared back in the kitchen chair and crossed my legs. The only thing missing was a forty-ounce and some Mary Jane.

"Let me ask you somethin', li'l miss project queen," Aunt Cookie said, invading my personal space and damn near smothering me with her bosom. "Who is you talkin' to? You payin' bills in this piece? Let me inform you, ain't no cussin' up in this mu'fucker, 'cause you is a chile! And another thing, don't no boostin', no drugs, and no raids go on up in here, 'cause we work every day! And any nigga that uses his hand to beat you gets cut the fuck up! You understand?" she said, moving so far into my personal space that I ended up falling backward out the chair.

Immediately I jumped up and started yelling and screaming for dear life! Living up the dramatics of being embarrassed, I started stomping my feet and banging on the walls. Before I could run and break something, Aunt Cookie was back in my face.

"Maybe you didn't hear me the first time," she said, bending down and looking at me. "Seems to be that you been a li'l grown ass, but from this point on, you is a chile. My chile.

Cookie Turner will bust a nigga's ass, so don't sleep. And another thing: When the bills come up in this mu'fucker, Cookie Jolene Turner or Boydon Brown's name is on 'em, and that's who payin' the bills up in here, not Vera. So, anytime you get to cussin', stompin', rollin' yo' eyes, or smellin' yo'self, think about how yo' Aunt Cookie love ya to death, but the next time you try and be Teena Marie up in this piece, hollering and shit, yo' Aunt Cookie will do a Rick James pimp-slap summersault on yo' ass! Understand?"

Aunt Cookie held her hand out and turned me so that I could face the living room window and said, "Go outside and be a li'l girl. Go play! 'Cause if you fuck around wit' me, cussin' and shit, I'ma tap dat ass. It's two li'l girls across the street. Get that jump rope over there, play and make some friends."

Not wanting to press my luck, I gathered my attitude, grabbed the jump rope, and went out the door. That's when I went on the block and met Shannon and Lee, bustin' out a street dance called a step.

"Oooh, Miss Dorsey Anna said ah East, ah West, I met my boyfriend at the candy store. He brought me ice cream, he brought me cake, he brought me home with a belly ache."

At first I was scared and didn't want to say anything. I thought that everybody probably knew that Grandma died of dope, and that Rowanda Wright was a chickenhead, so I stood silent, and while Shannon and Lee took turns with the street dance, I sang the tune in my mind.

"Ms. Cookie yo' mama?" Shannon asked, looking me up and down and then twisting her mouth like she already knew the truth.

"My mama? I ain't got no mama. All I got is me and my Aunt Cookie."

"You ain't got no mama? Everybody has got a mama."

"Well, I just told you that I ain't had no mama. I'm from the Lincoln Street Projects, and if you mess with me, I will beat yo' ass!"

"You cuss?" Lee asked, scared and shaking like she had never heard the word "ass" before.

Hell, I thought, *here was another one that didn't want me to cuss, but what was I supposed to say?* I thought that everybody cussed. Cussin' was nothing to me. Not only did I cuss, but I could tell 'em how to take the seeds out a nickel bag of weed. I could show 'em how to cook up coke with boiling water and a spoon. How to tie a belt and pull it tight around Grandma's arm while she said, "Grandma just need this to be well. Grandma just need this." I could show 'em anything that they needed to know, and all they could think to ask was, did I cuss?

"What the fuck you think? And furthermore, y'all don't even know me to be steppin' to me like that!"

"You crazy," Shannon said, waving me off. "You crazy."

I stood there for a moment, quiet and embarrassed, thinking about how Aunt Cookie was gonna bust my ass if she knew I was out here cussin'. So, I twisted my lips and told them that I could play double dutch.

"See, I got a rope," I said, tilting my head down, trying not to cuss, hoping they would accept my peace offering.

"I'm goin' first!" Lee screamed, yanking the rope from my hand.

"No you're not!" Shannon shouted. "Because I got zero no higher!"

And from that day on, it was every day outside with Shannon and Lee. Aunt Cookie had taught me early to keep my girlfriend circle tight, "'Cause hanging around a buncha women is a surefire way," Aunt Cookie would say, "to keep a buncha he-said-she-said bullshit going on." Therefore, my best friends never changed, and soon me, Shannon, and Lee graduated from double dutch to double dates.

And soon after that, we became women, individual women who loved each other like sisters yet were different, with different views, different ways of dealing with life, and a thousand different ways we each handled men.

And, if I may set the record straight, now that we're grown, Lee gets on my goddamn nerves like you wouldn't believe. She's an elementary school teacher, and she thinks that she has all the answers, when in actuality, she doesn't know shit.

Lee was raised by her mother and grandmother. Her daddy died when she was a baby, which made Lee, with the exception of me, the oldest little kid on the block. The only difference was I knew Rowanda Wright was a chickenhead, but Lee's ghost was up for grabs, which was probably why Lee cried all the time. If you looked at her wrong, she cried. If you coughed too loud, she cried. If she thought you didn't want to be her friend, she cried again. She wasted so many tears on nonsense that by the time she became adult, there were no more tears left and she started holding shit in. Now she's an adult with no common sense.

Now Shannon. Shannon owns a small magazine called *Girlfriends*, and believe me when I tell you Shannon got it goin' on! She knows how to handle her business, and her magazine is doing quite well. That's why she's my main girl, because she knows how to handle her own and she's not sitting around beggin' no man for shit!

Shannon was, and has always been, my ace boon coon! I could tell Shannon that I have screwed half of the NYPD and she wouldn't bat an eye. She would just say, "How big was the dick?" Shannon and I have been through it all, and I wouldn't trade any of the pain, the heartache, the headache, and even the times we don't get along, for nobody.

The only thing with Shannon is she can't play the game long enough to win. Love cheats her ass every time, and no matter what I say, she keeps getting caught. I explained to her to allow a big dick to be exactly what it is: a big dick. It is not companionship or commitment; it doesn't equate to love or even a strong like. It is what it is: plain, out-n-out dick.

Now, let me introduce Angie. Angie actually started out as Shannon's friend that she met while they were in college at Fisk. Shannon was the only one who went out of state to college, and when she came back, she brought an inno- cent-looking, but loud-mouth Southern gal who talked mo' shit than anybody I knew.

At first I was sort of reluctant to get to know her, but after me and Angie had to bust a bitch's ass for fuckin' with Shannon's man, I saw that Angie was a down-ass chick, and we been fly ever since, which has been close to ten years now. Ain't nobody like Angie, believe me. Angie is my road dawg!

I could tell Angie that I sucked a dick until the skin came off, and she would want instructions. Now, Angie may act innocent and sound sweet, but she is sneaky as hell. Don't put nothing pass Angie, 'cause she's got O.P.P. down to a science. She's the chick that will steal yo' man and have him sitting in your face with a look that said, "Now what?" That's how she got her job at the museum.

Angie is an art director for the Metropolitan Museum of Art in Manhattan, but Shannon told me that Angie has a music degree and lap-danced her way into the job. Angie was a secretary at the museum, and she started having an affair with the very married chairman of the board. The next thing we know, Miz Thing is over at the Met runnin' shit. The fucked up part about it is that Angie used to eat lunch with his wife every day, because the wife also worked at the museum.

Don't get it confused, though. Angie's shit has a limit, as there are unwritten rules among true blue girlfriends. Rule number one: It doesn't matter if the nigga had three teeth, a lopsided grin, and a dry curl; if your girlfriend at one time ever had him, wanted him, fucked him and flaunted him, then he is forever considered off limits. Therefore, Angie may steal a man, but he's never from the girlfriends' circle. Now, you, on the other hand, would have to watch yo' man. Understand?

Now me, when it comes to men, I no longer have much of a problem, 'cause Vera's got a "street-sophical" way of looking at the dating shit. Check this: When you date a man and he picks you up, make it your business to try to get to his house. Check out the scene, and if he acts suspicious, play it cool. All things fall into place. If he's talking sweet but he shows no action, dump him right away, 'cause he's a waste of time. If he has a job, but always has an excuse why he has no money, then he's useless. Can his ass. If he's flashing his money and talking about what he can do as if he's the pimp of the United States Mint, then sock it to him. Get all up in his pockets and drain his ass, 'til he learns to shut the fuck up. By the time that happens, get rid of him, 'cause he'll start complaining about spending too much money and needing to place you on a budget. He ain't yo' daddy; he just some dick, so toss him to the side. But, when the big dawg gets up in da house, starts running the game, and you find yourself submitting to his command because your heart's beating heavy, and you starting to get all giddy and laughing at stupid shit, then nine times out of ten, yo' ass is in love and headed for trouble. Which is why I keep my commitment level at zero and no longer lend myself to being in love and stuck on stupid. That way, I don't spend enough time to get to know how he thinks, how he feels, or what his dreams are. Love is not in my game plan, but gold-diggin', on the other hand, is always up for discussion.

That's how I hooked up with the old man, Roger. Well, sort of. Actually, he was the captain of the arresting officer when I was a criminal, on the run, and didn't even know it.

Let me tell you. It was a routine traffic stop, one where every third car gets pulled over. Well, guess who was the third car? You got it, ole girl. Anyway, Shannon was with me, and I gave the officer my registration and insurance card. Five minutes later, the officer asked me to please step out of the car.

"Excuse me?"

"Ma'am, please step out of the vehicle. And you too, ma'am," he said to Shannon.

This mu'fucka started reading me my rights, and Shannon started raising hell, yelling and screaming, acting like a damn fool. I could have kicked her ass! Straight up, 'cause she was making the situation worse. Next thing I knew, both of us were in handcuffs.

Now the heifer wants to cry. "But, what I do? What I do?"

Not to mention, it was a Friday, and guess what? As far as I knew, the courts didn't open 'til Monday. And what was I arrested for? A damn parking ticket that I forgot to pay that turned into a warrant. Shannon was arrested for throwing a punch at an officer.

When we got to the station, Shannon was like Sybil and turned on me. "I'm taking a plea bargain," she cried, with snot dripping from her nose. "I need to see the D.A."

"Shut up!" I said to her, giving her ass the evil eye. We were handcuffed to the hard wooden bench on the side of the processing officer's desk. "You don't need to see the D.A.," I said. "They should release yo' ass on a technicality called Cry Baby!"

"Fuck you! That's why I'm turning state's evidence on yo' ass! Anything they ask me, you did it. Oh, Lord Jesus!" And she started wailing again.

Then this fine-ass, distinguished older gentleman, dressed in black dress pants with a black-and-beige rayon shirt, walks over and asks Shannon does she want a tissue, and this crazy bitch starts telling him her life story. Once she's done crying on his shoulder, he turns to me and says, "What's up with you?"

I tried to put on the best seductive *sistafied* voice that I could muster up and said, "Baby, it's really a misunderstanding. I thought I paid the ticket."

"Ticket?" he asked.

"Yes, a ticket. Look, green, orange, brown, whatever the hell color prisoners are rocking these days, it doesn't suit me well. Please, can't I just pay the ticket?"

"Well, if it's a traffic ticket," he said, like I was the stupidest person on Earth, "then you will be going to night court. Pay the ticket and then you can leave."

"Yeah," I said, like I knew that all along, "but Assata Shakur over here tried to beat the officer up!"

He laughed and said, "I'll take care of that. By the way, what's your name?"

"Vera."

"Roger," he said, writing his phone number down on a piece of paper and then undoing the handcuffs that connected us to the wooden bench.

And from that point, it was on and poppin'! Now, granted, he's a little older than the guys I normally deal with, but his ass ain't ancient. He's fifty-five, and he got a dick like a damn horse. The first time he hit it, I was like, *What the hell is this? Turn the lights on let the freak out!* So, when I saw that the old man had it going on, I let him hit it all kinda ways, front, back, side, sixty-nine, whatever! 'Cause not only was I getting my shit off, I was counting all my gifts with every move. If he wanted to hit it from the back, I knew that had to be a mortgage payment. When I let him hit it from the side, with one leg against the wall and the other touching the floor, and he had my fat ass stretched out like the hum of a Negro spiritual, I knew I had my taxes paid, a new fur coat, two pair of Manolos, and a Chanel bag. And for the bonus, if he got his dick sucked, that meant that girlfriend had a bankroll like a legalized ho on the stroll! Hot damn!

And yes, he's married, but shit, when did his marriage become any of my concern? As long as he's lining my pockets, and life is lovely for me, then what his wife does with him is her business and not minc.

The first married man I slept with knocked my ass up three times. I played the soft and innocent role, like I was a virgin and just didn't know. So, every time I got pregnant and he thought about how he was the councilman of the South Ward in Newark and that it would raise a lot of concern and controversy if someone investigated why he spent so many nights in Manhattan, he would give me the money for an abortion and pay for a semester for me to go to school. Hell, I played his ass, fucked him day and day, night and day. Fucked him all the way to a 4.0 and a B.A. And, as a side, I screwed his assistant and made him pay for cosmetology school. Hell, I'm not stupid!

I always knew that I wanted to be a hairstylist, but I never had any plans on being Boomshika, doin' hair in the shop on the corner. Hell no! I wanted to be on Madison Avenue with the bougie-queens. I wanted to run shit. I wanted a spot so fly that when Oprah came in town, she knew my shop was the place to be.

So, I fucked for my money, and not no small-time money. I fucked the big bucks: congress-men, councilmen, CEOs, and vice presidents. If they were married, that was all the better, because then they went home at night. I didn't have to worry about them being up in my house, up in my face, and up in my business! Hell, they could spend Christmas with the wife and the kids, and I could continue to do my thing.

Now, I had been caught. I can't lie. Caught by the biggest player of them all—love. Love was just like life: a mu'fucka. Love had snatched my ass so fast that I didn't know whether I was coming or going. One day I was playing the big dick, and the next thing I knew, the big dick was playing me, had me dreaming about cooking, cleaning, going to the shop and coming straight home. I had almost lost my gold-diggin' shovel, and most recently, Taj Bennet has been the cause.

Taj is six foot even, with the blackest skin that anyone could imagine. His eyes have the persuasion of him being Asian, but his lips are full, and his nose is regal like an African royal. His hair flows with soft and whimsical dreadlocks that he wears in one ponytail pulled to the back, near the nape of his neck. The hair on his face, his mustache and beard, simply lays on his skin, and everything about him is well groomed. Taj is so fine that all I can say is "Goddamn!"

Last year, 2003, shortly after my thirtieth birthday, I was in the shop by myself, preparing to close for the evening when Taj walked in. He was dressed in mint green scrubs, running Nikes, and a white overcoat that read MD.

"Do you cater to dreads?" he asked. I had to do a double take. He was so fine that I had to pinch myself and make sure this was real. I couldn't help but smile, and then I said to myself, *Stay calm. This man is a bit too chocolate for your hormones to control.*

I cleared my throat and said, "Depends on whose dreads they are."

"What if they were mine?" he replied nicely, checking me from head to foot.

"Then," I said, "I would tell you to have a seat and let me take care of you."

He took off his jacket and revealed his muscular biceps. My eyes traced the bulging veins going down his arms into his hands and stopping at his manicured fingertips.

After he sat down, waiting for me to wash his hair, I went into the supply room to take out the shea butter shampoo and conditioner. I thought I had some Victoria's Secret Vanilla Bean Body Glitter on the second shelf, but I didn't. So, I took some of the shea butter shampoo and rubbed it into my skin. This way when I bent over to wash his hair, he could smell the mixture of coconut oil and berries rising from my cleavage.

As I began to run my hands through his soft hair, I stared at his body, starting with the six pack imprint showing lightly through his shirt;

then I massaged his thick thighs with my eyes, and by the time I stopped in the middle of his pants, that was all she wrote. I had to have this man.

"You like looking in my eyes, don't you?" I said, caressing his hair with the palms of my hands.

"I'm trying to see what they say," he replied.

"My eyes?"

"Yes."

"Why my eyes?"

"Because they let me see your heart."

I was silent the rest of the time that I did his hair. When I was done and he was preparing to leave, he said, "I'm diggin' you, and I have been for a while."

"You're diggin' me?" I smiled.

"Hell, yeah. Look at you. You bad as hell, and you run this place all by yourself. Sure, you have your assistants, but I see you here early in the morning and late at night, handling your business. Not to mention that you're one of the prettiest sisters that I've met in a long time."

"Thank you." I said, while trying to stop myself from blushing. "Look," Taj said, "I work at the hospital across the street.

Why don't we meet for latte in the morning, and after my shift, maybe we can go out. I would love to spend some time with you."

So, I tried it, the latte and the date, but his ass was a bit too deep for me. Too much god-damn cosmic energy, which is exactly why I chose to be his friend. Okay, let me stop lying, I fucked him a few times, but this was one time girlfriend couldn't hang. I couldn't keep up with the emotions that were racing a thousand miles per hour, and instead of the G-spot having the orgasm, my heart was the one shooting sparks.

"Listen, Taj," I said a year after we met, while lying in my king-sized sleigh bed with my back to his chest. "You and I can only be friends. I made myself a promise long time ago to never date my clients, and I should have stuck to it."

He pressed his chest closer into my back.

"What's the problem, Vera?" he asked.

"Did I say there was a problem?" I said with a smirk.

"Do you ever say you have a problem?"

"Don't answer a question with a question."

"Then answer mine first," he insisted, bracing my shoulders and turning me so we were face-to-face, exchanging breaths.

"There are a lot of things that you don't understand. Look, I'm seeing somebody."

"What?"

"Yes, and I just need that kind of space. Seeing you and spending time with you is not good for me or my other relationship."

"Other relationship? Vera, you're full of shit! You need to stop lying to yourself and face the fact that you love me."

Love him, I thought. Me love someone, other than Louie V., Chanel, Manolo Blahnik, my hair salon, Aunt Cookie, Uncle Boy, Shannon, Lee, and Angie? There was no one and nothing else left to love, other than the memory of Grandma's laugh, the one she had before the high wore off. The laugh that let us know it was okay to ask for something to eat or ask her to tell us her dreams about being clean.

The space for love was already crowded, and the thought of Taj trying to fit into this dimension felt asthmatic. "Can we just be friends?"

"And how long is that game supposed to be played? You're thirty-one years old and you're acting like a kid! Never mind," he said throwing the plum-colored chenille comforter off of him and reaching for his black Armani dress pants. "Fuck it! When you get it together and stop chasing dead dreams and somebody else's drug habit, let me know."

I lay in the bed and didn't move. I heard the door slam when he left. I tried to sleep, but the whistle of the October wind and the knocking of the tree branches against my bedroom window made too much noise. For the first time since I was eight years old, I missed the tranquility of the projects. There was no radio thumping from the apartment next door, no cussin', no Ms. Johnson, no strange men coming in and out of the house, and nobody to bang the man in the head that kept sneaking in Rowanda's bed.

When my thoughts became too heavy to handle, I jumped in my red X5 and drove. For the first time in twenty-three years, since I was taken away in a pink Aries K, I went to visit the Lincoln Street Projects. The first face that I saw was Rowanda. She stood still, squinted her eyes, and stared at me. The muscles in my throat clenched tightly. I hadn't seen her since I was nine, when I spit in her face and Aunt Cookie beat my ass.

I sat in my car and watched Rowanda watch me. Despite the fish frown that she had acquired from years of being in love with dope, she looked identical to me. There she stood, watching me with my eyes, my hands, and with the same brown-sugar color in her skin. She watched me and she smiled.

I left her standing there. I left her crooked lean, rotten teeth, and her smile standing there watching me as if she knew me, as if she and I were familiar with one another. I hated this bitch, and there she stood, crooked, nodding out but watching me, tilted to the side, but never touching the ground, giving the illusion that one leg was shorter than the other. Standing there as if I belonged to her, forcing me to remember why I spit on her.

When I returned home and parked on my dimly lit street, I saw Taj sitting on my front stoop. I was relieved as hell that he was there, despite the fact that we had just had an argument.

"Where'd you go?" Taj said as I walked up the steps. His white polo shirt was half open, and his tie hanging loose around his neck.

"I went home," I said, walking up the steps and standing in front of him.

"Why'd you do that?" he asked.

"Because I needed to find me."

"Did you find you?" he said, pulling me close and placing his arms around my waist.

"No," I admitted. "Instead, I found a buncha dopefiends and their memories. I heard too many voices, and I saw too many faces."

"You know I can't leave you, Vera."

"Then just be my friend. There's no room for anything else."

He bent down and pressed his forehead softly into my stomach and said, "You know you don't mean that."

I shot his ass a look, shook off the electric sparks that his hands were shooting up my thighs, took my heart out, and had a talk. I said, just like Aunt Cookie used to tell me when I was a kid and went to the grocery store, "I don't care how much you like it, or how much you beg, don't look at shit, don't touch shit, and don't try to convince me of shit, 'cause you ain't gettin' shit."

Taj was beginning to tap into a part of my life that I couldn't control, so, in an effort to maintain my composure and keep myself from crying every day, I knew I had to let him go.

Hold on now. You know we're just getting started, so sit back, relax, and get yo'self a drink or two, 'cause I got some Spike Lee, Hollywood, Oprahfied shit fo' yo' ass.

Step One

"I'ma cut the nigga!" a harsh and cold female voice said into the receiver as I struggled to hold the phone to my ear. It was three o'clock in the morning, and Taj's raspy voice, breathing heavy in my ear, asking me, "Who is it?" didn't help any.

Then I heard it again, "I'ma cut the nigga!" and then she hung up. The caller ID said the number was unavailable, and *69 said that whoever was gonna "cut the nigga" was out of the area. I said a quick prayer and hoped that whoever got sliced would survive.

Two hours later, the phone rang again. Taj was looking at me like I was disrespecting him and shit, talking about, "You need to tell ole boy that when I'm up in the spot, to tame his midnight phone calls." Despite the fact that Taj was super fine, I was this close to tellin' him to shut the fuck up, but the recorded operator interrupted my thoughts, informing me that I was receiving a collect call from an inmate in the county jail.

Immediately, I wanted to know what the hell was going on. The last time I dated a nigga in jail, he was ballin'. I had beat him for his money, and he was calling to inform me that when he "hit the brick after doing a twenty-year stint" he was going to come back and kill my ass. After him, I left them ballin' mu'fuckers alone and moved onto the niggas that were more apt to commit white-collar crimes. Whoever it was on my phone calling collect from the county jail, it was beyond me.

When it came time for the person to state their name, all I heard was the same unknown female voice that called earlier say, "Come get me!" And then, when I pressed two for the person to repeat her name, she said, "Right now, goddamnit, Babygirl!" That's when I realized that it was Aunt Cookie. Immediately I jumped out of the bed and left Taj, and his hard-on waiting for me.

When I got to the precinct, it was six o'clock in the morning. I hadn't seen the inside of this place since Shannon and I were arrested over a year ago. I walked in and asked the officer at the desk what the charges and bail were for Cookie Turner.

"Assault with a deadly weapon," is what the officer said as he looked on his computer screen. "Yep," he said, pointing to the screen but looking in my face. "Assault. She lucky he didn't kick her ass, is all I got to say."

"Well, nobody asked you what you had to say."

He rolled his eyes and informed me that Aunt Cookie's bail was five thousand dollars cash. No exceptions.

No exceptions, I thought. *No exceptions? Humph, we'll see about that.* I stepped away from the counter where the officer was, flipped open my cell phone, and hit speed dial.

"Roger?"

"No, Roberta."

"Roberta?" Oh, his wife. She had answered Roger's cell phone. "Excuse me, but is Roger available?"

"Maybe I should ask you."

"Excuse me?"

"Excuse you? Excuse you? Excuse you for which time? The time where you had my husband and he missed his daughter's graduation? Or excuse you for the time I waited at home with candles and dinner and my husband tripped over my bed and fell into yours?

"Look, hun, perhaps you have me mistaken for someone else, but as far as I know, your husband loves you too much to be tripping over you and falling for someone else," I said, lying like a damn dog. "Do you need to talk? Is something wrong?"

"Listen, don't patronize me!" she shouted.

"Patronize you? Sweetheart, from what I can see, your husband thinks of nothing but you." Then I hit her with the famous line, "Roger and I are just friends."

"Oh," she said, sounding as if she were taken aback. "Well, you just remain friends, because he is my man. In any event, he isn't here, but I'm sure that at some point, if you're to be reached, he'll find you."

Oh, no this bitch didn't! Now see, if I ain't need a favor from Roger, I woulda blew up her whole spot. I just about gagged at the thought of biting my tongue and spitting out this one: "I'ma pray for you, because I'm sure that you're much too beautiful to be worried over Roger like this. You take care, Roberta." *Wit' yo' stupid ass!*

"Excuse me," I said, stepping back to the counter where the officer was. "Is Captain Roger Sims due to come in?"

"Captain Sims? Is he here? Yeah, this is his shift, but he doesn't wanna see you."

This mu'fucker was working my last nerve. "Can you please call Captain Sims?"

"Well, since you said please."

A few minutes later, Roger appeared with his back arched, like he actually had some backbone and wasn't the same li'l weak link that liked his dick sucked and his asshole played with. The thought of that made me snicker. He actually looked good. He still seemed old, but he looked nice. It had been a month since I gave him the time of day, and I was sure that he would want some pussy when this was all over with, but I would have to cross that bridge when I got to it.

Roger was dressed in a pair of black dress pants with a light blue shirt. His gun sat in a black leather holster, resting on the side of his hip. When he saw me, he gave me a brief overview and then he smirked, seeming somewhat annoyed. What the fuck could be his problem? I was the one that should be pissed off!

"What did you say to my wife?" he said, motioning for me to step to the back and into his office.

"Excuse me? What did you say?"

"You heard me. What did you say to my wife?"

"Your wife? I didn't say anything out of the way to your wife."

"Then why is she crying, screaming, and packing my shit as we speak?"

"I wouldn't know that, honey. I told her that you loved nobody but her and that she needed to be certain of that."

"That's what you told her?"

"Yes."

"Then why is she calling me a cheat?"

"Roger, baby," I said, about to choke, "I wouldn't do anything to mess with your marriage. I'm not here for that."

"Then why are you here?"

"My Aunt Cookie got arrested."

"What?"

"Arrested, handcuffed, picked up."

"When?"

"Late last night, early this morning. I need you to get her out."

"I can't do that." He started walking away.

"Where are you going? I need you."

"You need me? You don't need me. You need a favor, as usual. I'm sick of that. I need more. I want you to be with me only. I've thought about leaving my wife, but I can't make that sacrifice until I know that you and me are going to be all right."

Leave his wife and live where? He must be stupid if he thinks I want his old ass laying up in my face every day.

"Baby, when that time comes, we'll deal with it."

"Deal with it? I have to deal with it now! My wife, I can go home and soothe her, but you, I can't seem to get a handle on you. It's been a month since we spent any quality time together. I want you to commit to me. I'm a grown man, and you playing me for a little boy. Don't fuck with me, Vera!" he said, pointing into my face. "Don't fuck with me!"

"Look, this is not the time or the place. I need you to help me, okay. We'll work something out. You're scaring me."

"I don't mean to scare you, but I don't like the way I've been treated."

"I'm sorry, okay? We'll talk, but I need you right now." Then I took him by the hand and massaged it with my palm, so he could feel the smooth heat from my skin.

"Officer Ryan," Roger said into the intercom on his phone, "was there a woman brought in here late last night or early this morning?"

"Yeah, Cookie Turner."

"What are the charges?"

"Domestic violence shit. She hit her boyfriend in the head with a bat."

"Did he file a complaint?"

"No. He insisted that he tripped and fell into the wall."

"What's the bail?"

"Five grand. Cash."

"Her bail's been posted. Let her out."

While I waited for Aunt Cookie to be released from the bullpen, little did Roger know that his ass was history. How dare he stand up there as if he were big shit and try to talk down to me? For a moment, I felt like I was ten again, and standing in front of me was Larry Turner, fully dressed in somebody's gray pinstriped Easter suit and derby hat.

Larry was an old man, old enough to be Rowanda's daddy, and he thought he was fine. He stood about six foot four inches, with salt-and-pepper hair, black tree trunk skin, with round and sagging eyes. His voice rattled when he spoke, and he called my name like he had a thing for it.

"That li'l bitch really had that chile, huh, Cookie?" I remember Larry asking when I was a little girl. He was sitting at the dinner table with a piece of chicken in his mouth, and his girlfriend eyeing me.

"What ole bitch?" Aunt Cookie asked, looking toward Larry's girlfriend. "This heifer over here, she pregnant?"

Larry clenched his mouth tight, and his jaw-bone stuck out. "I'm talkin' 'bout Rowanda."

"Oh, that's the bitch you talkin' about. Sometimes I get confused."

"How come nobody never told me that Rowanda had that baby?"

"'Cause you ain't need to know. What was you gonna do? Did the prison you was in have a daycare?"

"You kinda nasty," Larry's girlfriend said to Aunt Cookie, with her drawn-on eyebrows raised.

"Oh, hold on," Aunt Cookie responded. "Anybody know who this strumpet is? You best be quiet and mind yo' business. This between my brother and me."

"It's all right, Trish," Larry said to his girl-friend with a soft, mellow tone. He took out a cigarette, lit it, took a drag, and blew out the smoke.

"You talkin' down to me for some li'l dope-fiend's kid. This chile probably ain't even mine. Her mama is a ho. Who knows who the daddy really is?"

Everything fell off the table by the time Aunt Cookie ran toward Larry Turner, causing him to fall backward out of the chair. Aunt Cookie jumped on top of him and placed her elbow in his throat.

"I will cut you, nigga!" she screamed, with spit flying out her mouth. "I will slice yo' ass apart, mu'fucker!"

"Get off me, Cookie! You fuckin' bitch, get off me!"

"Oh, no, mu'fucker, you're the bitch! You ain't shit. You're worse than a fuckin' gutter rat! What kinda man wanna bust li'l girls' pussies open? You ain't shit, nigga!"

While trying to shake the thoughts from my mind, I kept hearing my name being called, and when I blinked my eyes, as if to bring myself back to present, Roger was standing in front of me. "Don't forget that we need to talk," he said, interrupting my thoughts. I blew him a fake-ass kiss and mumbled, "Catch that and kiss my ass with it."

I walked out the door, holding Aunt Cookie by the hand. When we got outside, I felt like slapping the shit out of her and knocking her old ass back to the 1974 time warp that her wardrobe was from. She stood there on the passenger side of my truck, with lips and eyes to match her attitude, like her shit didn't stink.

She was dressed in silver metallic go-go boots, a brown corduroy mini skirt, a leather patched jacket, and a pocketbook to match. No wonder they arrested her; she was in fashion violation. Sirens, water sprinklers, and all kinds of emergency devices probably started going off as soon as she hit the pavement! The NYPD didn't arrest her; they just held her over. It had to be the fashion police that got ahold of this shit, which only enhanced the fact that I was thoroughly disgusted with her.

I sucked my teeth, stomped my feet, and rolled my eyes at her as she entered my truck.

"Roll 'em again and you won't have 'em for long," Aunt Cookie said.

"What the hell you doin' getting arrested? What, there was nothing else you could do other than try and beat up Uncle Boy?"

"Beat up Uncle Boy? He lucky I ain't stone cold kick his ass!"

"What did he do, Aunt Cookie? What?"

"I caught him feeling on the barmaid's ass."

"What barmaid?"

"The one at the Fox Trapp. The same bitch I had to break his ass about before."

"So you had to beat him in the head? His goddamn knees were just too much. His freakin' head was all you could see? You lucky he didn't die!"

"Let me tell you somethin'. I ain't bring you in this world, but I brought you on this side of town, and I will shut yo' whole shit down if you say another mu'fuckin' cuss word at me! Now, cuss again!" she said, lunging her chest toward my face. "Bring it! You better take a break and recognize. You know how I do it!"

"You must like jail if you still threatening people."

"Shut up and let me talk. I ain't Rowanda. You ain't gonna out-mouth me. Your Uncle Boy, who you think is hot shit, was disrespecting me in the bar. I told him before we got there that if he fucked around, I would take the bat out my car and whoop his ass. He ain't believe me, so I had to show and prove."

"Show and prove what, Aunt Cookie? You been with the man for twenty somethin' years. What's the point?"

"The point is that I ain't the one, and that's what up! You feel me? Give yourself a chance to fall in love, and you'll see exactly what I'm talking about."

I tooted up my lips and said, "Love? Puh-leeze, Vera Wright-Turner will never take it there."

"Mm-hmm," Aunt Cookie said, opening the car door. "The mouth can always out-talk the heart, but best believe, what the heart want, the heart get. So save all that what-you-won't-do-for-love shit for somebody else, 'cause, I done lived long enough to know better." With that said, she switched her hips and slammed the car door.

Step Two

"All I said to Lee was that Mr. James was not all Lee thought he was cracked up to be, and she got pissed," I explained to Shannon, while she was yelling in my ear about some ole dumb shit and interrupting my conversation with Taj.

"You will apologize!" Shannon yelled.

"I will not!"

"You most certainly will! Your mouth is too big, and nobody asked for your opinion."

"Excuse me? But that nigga is not James Evans from *Good Times*, and Lee's ass ain't Florida."

"What does that have to do with the price of tea in China?"

"Nothing, but she ain't dating the black knight of the ghetto. She dating the pimp of the pulpit!" Then I hung up. I had to get back to the other line.

"You really need to get it together," Taj insisted.

He was right, but so what? "Listen, I've explained to you my situation. Hell, Taj, I'm doing you a favor."

"You're doing me a favor?"

"Yes."

"Please explain that."

"I could've just played you, but I didn't. I was straight up with you. Now, listen, I'm willing to be your friend, but the moment you get out of hand, I'ma have to let you know."

"Oh, so you don't care if I date somebody else?"

"Do you, boo."

"Really?"

"That's right. Do you. If you like it, I love it."

"Oh, so you're the master player?"

"Maybe so."

"Well, I don't like players."

"Humph," I said, sucking my teeth. "Don't hate the player, hate the game."

If Taj felt that he could date somebody else and they would be the freak of the week and the woman of his dreams all at the same time, then go for it!

I turned my radio on, put my feet up, and started singing, "Lipstick is great, ass is straight, and the X5 is outside!" Then I put a human beat box to the end of my song. "It won't be long 'fore Vera have it goin' on." The doorbell rang, and I did the Cabbage Patch, mixed with the whop, as I opened the door to see Roger standing there with a bouquet of red roses.

"I got us tickets for the Sade concert," Roger ouid, smiling and looking stupid.

"Sade?" I asked, totally stunned. Why wus he at my door? I hadn't called him. Nobody invited him over here. Tickets to see Sade? Was he serious? Going to a concert to see Sade is something you do with somebody you actually like, not somebody you just bangin'.

"Why'd you do that?" I asked.

"Because today is our one-year anniversary."

"Are you for real? One year anniversary for what?"

"Since we been together."

"Since we been together? We haven't been together. We been bonin' for twelve months, but we ain't been together for one day, let alone one year."

"You mean to tell me that all you care about is the sex?"

"Hell, no!" I wanted to say, "It's all about the Benjamins, baby!" but I figured that would be too much like slippin' on my game, so I decided to apologize and make up a lie about having a bad day. I told him that I just needed a few minutes to get dressed.

This man had it all laid out. There was a stretch X Caliber waiting outside my Brooklyn brownstone, with red carpet rolled from my front door to the feet of the European-dressed driver, who, may I add, looked better than a mu'fucker, especially for a white boy. If I could have positioned my hand just right, I would have tapped that ass while I was sliding into the car. Instead, I winked my eye and mouthed "call me" as he closed the door.

To start the night off, Roger gave me a pair of two carat diamond earrings. We went to Carnegie Hall and watched Sade turn the house out! I tried to get in the mood while Sade was singing, but I couldn't stop thinking about Taj, and Roger kept placing his hand on my damn knee! A couple of times, I gave Roger one of Aunt Cookie's looks that would usually shut 'em down, but not Roger. He was the Energizer bunny, and his mouth kept going and going and going.

This was too much, and when he suggested that we hit Tavern on the Green, I knew that he had officially lost it. Could he have forgotten that he was a married man? Maybe I should have reminded him that his real anniversary was the one that celebrated the day of his marriage to his wife, not me.

"Roger, why are you doing all of this?" I said as the waitress handed us menus.

"Vera, I can't believe you. Most women get all sentimental about things like this, but you're just like whatever."

"I don't need you to do all of this."

"Really?" he said, soft and sweet and making me sick at the same time. "That's the nicest thing that you've said to me in a long time."

"I mean it," I said. Then I thought to myself, *I don't need you to spend your money on me like this. I would much rather you spend it on that cowhide Chanel bag I've been eyeing at Neiman's.*

"Damn, Vera, you are so sweet," he said, looking deep into my eyes, as if he were actually sexy. "I knew you could be devoted to me. I have a question, though. How come you never call me on the weekends, and why are you always hanging out with your girlfriends? That needs to stop."

"Excuse me?"

"What's the problem?"

Roger, I thought to myself, *you old and gray-headed mu'fucker, please trust me enough to allow me to be screwing another nigga on yo' ass!* Then I looked at him, smiled, and said, "You are so much of a good man that I can't wait for the day when we'll be married and you'll be able to see how much you mean to me."

"Do you realize how beautiful you are?"

Before I could process how ridiculous he was sounding, I heard a voice that placed me in the mind of tranquility. When I looked up, Taj and some skinny little bag of bones chick were being escorted to the table directly across from where Roger and I were sitting.

"Excuse me, Roger," I said, sliding my chair from the table and standing to greet Taj and his friend.

"Hi," I said to the young lady as I gave her a quick overview. She had on Star Jones shoes, which were ran over and cheap, a Rainbow Shop polyester pantsuit—hmph, if only I had a match!—and her hair hadn't been done since 1981! I had this chick beat hands down. I arched my back and practically threw my titties in Taj's face.

"I'm Vera," I said, holding out my hand as a polite gesture.

"Oh," she said, seeming startled. "I'm Aiesha."

"Very nice to meet you. Interesting suit. What, Target?"

"I didn't catch who you were," the bitch said, pointing to herself and then to Taj. "I didn't catch who you were to either one of us."

"This is Vera," Taj said with a sly smile. "She's a very dear friend of mine."

A dear friend? "Oh, Taj," I said, sounding concerned. "This little date seems nice, but if you don't mind, Keisha."

"Aiesha," she said, correcting me.

"Whatever. Please sit here and talk to Roger for a moment. Roger, honey, I need just a second to tell Taj something. I don't want him to be embarrassed, so give me a moment to tell him this alone." Then I hit 'em both with a plastic-ass smile.

Stepping into the foyer, Taj asked, "May I help you?" sounding cocky as a mu'fucker, giving me the screw face. "What seems to be the problem?"

"What is all of this?" I asked.

"What is all of what?"

"The chick in the other room."

"Excuse me, but does 'don't hate the player, hate the game' sound remotely familiar to you?"

"Your point?"

"My point?" He chuckled. "You made these rules. Now, let me explain this to you, when you say something, you have to be comfortable with the delivery and the reception. Therefore, when you made your little player comment, you left the door wide open. Understand?"

"Yes, but—"

"No buts," he said, cutting me off. "We're being rude to our guests, so if you don't mind, I'd like to get back to my party." He winked his eye, threw on his best Billy Dee voice, and said, "*Ciao, bella.*"

After dinner, I went home and got right in the bed. I tossed and turned for hours. I thought the heat was up too high, causing me to sweat, so I turned the heat off, despite the fact that it was January. I changed my nightie at least three times, but the smoothness of the change in the material, or the prettiness of color, made no difference. I was uncomfortable from the inside out, and for the first time, I was willing to admit that I was upset.

What did they talk about? I wondered. Did he tell her how he grew up on South Fourteenth Street with Malik, Kaareem, Raheem, John, and Big Stuff? Did he tell her how Taniesha was his first girlfriend, but she joined the army and left him for Uncle Sam? Did he tell her how his mother died but left a spirit so strong, that she raised him and his siblings from the grave, while his father helped along?

And, if they didn't talk, did they make love? Did he hold her the same way he held me, tight and close, like running waters? Did he whisper to her and call her his Almond Joy?

I got up, sat in my oversized Laura Ashley recliner, and looked out the window. The last thing I remembered before hearing the phone ring and realizing that I had fallen asleep in the recliner was how pretty the sun looked sneaking into the sky. "Yes?" I said, answering the phone.

"You're still up?" It was Taj.

"No, I've been 'sleep all night," I said, lying, but relieved to hear his voice. I was forcing myself to sound indifferent.

"I was thinking about you," he said.

"Really?" I snapped. "Was that before or after ole girl left your apartment?"

"Would it bother you if she just left?"

"Not at all."

I could hear him smiling. "Open the door."

"What?"

"Open the door. I'm outside."

When he walked in, he immediately stepped into my personal space, and he continued until I bumped my head against the wall and had nowhere to turn. His breath was hot and heavy, and I enjoyed the radiance. I was melting with each word, with each touch. My nipples were erect, and my vagina had relaxed, waiting for him to take over.

He placed both of his arms on the sides of my head, resting his hands on the wall. Softly kissing me on the lips, he said, "So, are you ready to change your standards?"

"No."

"Why are you lying?"

"I'm not."

"Stop it."

"Stop what?"

"Stop lying and tell the truth. It's a lot sexier when you tell the truth." His breathing was rapid, and he was smelling of Cool Water as he started kissing me on my neck.

"What are you doing?" I asked.

"Exactly what you need me to do."

Step Three

"You know I can rap," Taj said out of the clear blue, and for no reason in particular, other than to hear himself speak. I think he liked the sound of his own voice. Why else would he say some stupid shit about how he liked to rap?

"That's really nice. I guess in your human beat box days they called you M.C. the M.D.?"

"Hilarious! Do you think I have been a doctor all my life?"

"Yeah."

"Please. You don't know the half of it."

"Half of what? What, you used to sling rocks? What were you, a baller? Please, Taj."

"And if I was, I wouldn't tell you. Yo' ass would sell me out in five minutes."

"Oh, no you didn't. I'm a down-ass chick."

He cracked up laughing, but I didn't think the shit was funny. He said, "You are so corny. You have outgrown the project shit, so stop tryin' to be down."

"Anyway," I said, nixing his comment, "what half don't I know?"

"My better half. She's in Newark with my three kids."

My heart dropped. "What? What kind of game are you playing?"

"Aw, I peeped your card, caught you caring about the game."

"Look, what's your point? I'm laying up here in the bed with you, naked, and all you can think to say is a buncha stupid shit!"

"What's the problem? I thought you liked it that way."

"What way?"

"Games and shit. Zero commitment."

"I never said anything about games, but zero commitment, yeah, I can dig that."

"Then why would you care if I have a wife and kids?"

Usually I didn't care, but this time was different. "Do you have a wife and kids?"

"No."

"Then there's no point to this conversation."

"There is a point."

"What?"

"You're in love with me."

"In love with you? Negro, please! Let me tell you what I love. See, the new Louie V. Japanese

Line, I love that, the new Manolos with the water colors and the embroidered beads, I love those."

"Oh, so you're shallow?"

"No, I'm just not committable."

"Why not?"

"I'm just not."

"But why not?"

He was beginning to push my buttons and piss me off. "Look, what are you driving at? You want me to love you, fine, I love you. But I got a crackhead for a mother, a child molester for a father, and a humdinger that raised me. Take it or leave it."

"Me take it or leave it? You have to decide that. All I want is you."

"That's a part of me."

"It may be who you've been, but it doesn't have to control who you are. Do you think you're the only person that had it rough? What do you think South Fourteenth Street in Newark is, the suburbs? You really don't know the half of it. The ghetto is filled with dreams. From the dopefiend to the bum on the street, everybody has a dream, but it's up to you to make your dream come true.

"Hell, nobody would've thought that Taj Bennett would be somebody's doctor. Vera, let me inform you, I was slingin' rock and paying for medical school at the same time. What kinda shit was that? I was trying to save lives, and all the while selling shit that would take 'em away. And to top that off, my mother was dead. My brother and sister don't even remember her."

"At least you have memories of a mother. I had two fiends trying to raise me!"

"How'd you feel about that?"

"How'd I feel? Hell, wasn't everybody but the schoolteacher and the social worker fiends? Please, you have to be shown different to know different, and living with an old-ass dopefiend who shot up the welfare check and the food stamps ain't no picnic."

"Why not?"

"Why not? Why not? Because in a dopefiend's world, they don't give a fuck about you. Children have to be born grown, and the only stops they are allowed to make is to get off the bottle and learn how to go to the potty, otherwise, they are an inconvenience. Do you know how many times I have heard, 'Vera, you fuckin' up my high! Go sit down. You ain't that hungry'?"

"How many times?"

"For eight years! Eight fuckin' years!"

"And then what?"

"Then Aunt Cookie came and she loved me, no matter what."

"No matter what?"

"Yes, no matter what. No matter how many nights I stole food and hid it in my room. No matter how many nights I cried to see Rowanda."

"Why did you cry to see Rowanda?"

"Because I thought I needed her."

"Why?"

"I don't wanna talk about it."

"Why not?"

"Because I can't."

The room went silent, and deep in my mind I could hear Rowanda cry. I could hear her when she said, "I'd rather be dead then to have a man bust a nut in my baby's bed!" And when she found Grandma naked and bleeding, she swore to me that she would never leave. She swore that she would always be here, and she lied. She lied. I tried not to let too much snot drip from my nose as I cried into the hairs on Taj's chest.

He rubbed my back and said, "All you gotta do is let it go, baby. All you gotta do is let me in."

"Roger," I said the next morning, getting directly to the point, while I was giving myself a fresh pedicure, "you are not coming over here."

"But why not?"

"Because I said no!"

"You know, Vera, when I get a moment to catch you, I'ma break yo' ass! You starting that shit again."

"What shit again?"

Just as I said that, Taj came out of the bathroom wrapped in a towel, and he had his cell phone to his ear.

Who the hell is he talking to? Is he trying to play me for stupid? I know he's not disrespecting me by talking to no other chick while he's in my house.

"Roger, I gotta go. Call me later. Smooches. Taj, who are you talking to?"

"Excuse me? Who am I talking to? Well, it certainly isn't Roger."

"You heard my conversation?"

"Yeah, I heard you, but it's all good. Which is exactly why I'ma step and give you the space you need to play this cat and mouse game."

"Cat and mouse game? You the one mackin' on the line in my bathroom!"

"Baby, let me tell you something," he said, taking off his towel and rubbing baby oil across his chest and into his nipples. "I don't have to play those games. If I want to talk to a young lady, I don't need your permission. And for your information, I was checking my voice mail. But you check this, don't disrespect me again, because I don't play that shit. I got the player's hustle down pat, so stop trying to play me, because if I gave it back, yo' ass would break!

"Now, I may be a doctor, but I can be just as ghetto as you are, so don't be fooled. And believe this when I tell you, the next time you try and play me, you can kiss me, my friendship, and the tolerance I have for your ass good-bye!"

"Excuse me?"

"Excuse you? Well, maybe this time, but the next time you try and play me for stupid by talking to some other man while I'm here, I won't be returning. You understand?"

"Yes," I responded out of shock and surprise. Had I just been read? And if my genital area wasn't soaked and wet from the ambiance of being told what to do, my feelings would've been hurt. But shit, I had to hit this nigga off right then and right there, 'cause he had my coochie all the way live!

I didn't say a word. I just stood in front of him and slowly slid the straps of my black silk nightie off my shoulders, revealing the beauty of my 38Cs, and then I straddled across his lap, making him lay back and allowing him to feel as if he had been hand delivered to the moon.

"You know, baby," Taj said after I finished wearing his ass out, "making love to you is sweet as hell, but I'm out. I'll call you in a few days."

"What?" That was usually my line. What the hell was he talking about? "What did you say?"

"I said I'll call you in a few days."

"And why is that?"

"Excuse me? Didn't you just tell me not that long ago that I shouldn't hate the player?"

"Yeah."

"Well, then I'm taking your advice."

"But."

"No buts, baby. Plus, you just tried some ole ghetto slick shit, and I didn't appreciate it."

"Well."

"No wells."

Oh, this mu'fucka was 'bout to piss me the fuck off! How the hell was he tryin' to act like I didn't just get finished knockin' his ass down? And now that he done conveniently came all over the place and got my coochie filled with so much cum that my ovaries were probably drowning, he thought that he could look me in my face and say that he'd call me in a few days? Oh, I don't think so, 'cause Vera don't roll like that!

"Look, Taj," I said, letting him know that I was pissed the hell off.

"Look Taj what?"

"Stop cutting me off, goddamnit!" He shot my ass a look. "Didn't I just say that I was sorry?"

"You said you were sorry? Vera, please, who you think you talking to? This is Taj, baby."

"I know who you are."

"Well, then you should know that you didn't apologize to me."

"What do you think all of what just happened between us was?"

"Sex."

"Sex?"

"Sex. Sweet-ass, soaking wet, bustin'-a-nut sex. That's it. But I'm with you, baby. You're a freak to the core, and if you played the other part of your game correctly, the part where I like to be treated nice and more like your man, then we would be straight. However, if for one minute you think that you can talk to another brotha in my presence and all you have to do is hit me off, then you really don't know who you're messing with."

Oh, no his ass didn't. I'm mistaken, right? This fool done stole all my lines. What the hell was this?

Before I finished my thought, Taj reached over me, grabbed his clothes, got dressed, and walked out of the room.

"When should I expect to hear from you again?" I heard my dumb ass yelling.

"We'll talk," he yelled back.

"We'll talk?"

"Yeah, baby. My hair appointment for you to twist my dreads is Thursday."

"Hair appointment? Thursday? It's Sunday!"

"Very good, baby." And the nigga left.

Fuck him, though. Vera got this.

It had been three days, and I couldn't continue to take this. Was this what was called being in the doghouse? Was this nigga playing me? But you know what? Fuck him! Yeah, fuck him! Vera got this.

I ran some bath water, splashed in some Bath and Body Works' raspberry bath oil, lay back, turned on the shower radio, and closed my eyes. WBLS was playing the Quiet Storm and Natalie Cole (of all goddamn people) was singing about how to keep a good man, 'cause all of sudden she's catching hell.

As soon as she went off, here comes Xscape singing "Who Will I Run To." I had to laugh. Why the hell is a group named Xscape singing about who will they run to? Hell, just leave. Get it? Escape!

Oh my God, and this was the killer, Whitney Houston's, "Saving All My Love for You"! Oh, no she didn't! Whitney had officially lost her damn mind. She was gonna have to save her love, 'cause Bobby couldn't stay the fuck outta jail. I knew I had a lot of nerve, but these brokenhearted bitches were gonna have to shut the fuck up!

Before I could turn the radio off, the phone rang. While getting up to answer the phone, I couldn't quite lift my leg up high enough, so I tripped getting out of the tub and slid on the floor.

"Hello?" I said, trying not to sound desperate.
"Vera," Roger said, "listen."

I said this nice and slow, "What . . . the . . . fuck . . . do . . . you want?"

"Hold the hell up. Why are you talking to me like this?"

I just hung up and jumped back in the tub. I couldn't stop thinking about Taj. Technically, I should've been mad as hell, but I was trying to be a big girl about the situation and not sweat it. I must admit your girlfriend was pissed.

Just then the phone rang again. I got out the tub, grabbed a towel, and answered the phone.

"Hello?" It was a telemarketer. What the fuck! To hell with this. I had more things to do than to be soaking in the tub and thinking about Taj. Hell, he wasn't my man.

An hour into doing absolutely nothing, I lay on the chaise in my bedroom and pressed play on the DVD. I decided to watch *Love Jones*, which was totally the wrong move, because as soon as Lorenz Tate started reciting poetry, I got pissed the fuck off. But I was forced to watch the whole movie. What else was there to do?

I thought I heard the phone ringing, but when I picked it up, I realized it was the phone on the TV. Then I thought I heard the doorbell ringing, and when I jumped my fat ass up to answer the door, I realized that it was for the brownstone next door. Instantly, I got pissed off. That's when I could have sworn that the phone was ringing again, but then I thought about how, technically, the shit hadn't rang but twice since last night, and it was now six o'clock in the morning, so my phone must have been broken.

I called the operator and said, "Hello, this is Vera Wright-Turner." I gave her my phone number. "Uh, my phone isn't working."

"Really? What seems to be the problem?" the operator said.

I realized at that point that I had officially lost my mind. "Sorry to bother you. It seems to be okay now." I hung up the phone and then called Shannon.

"Hey, Shannon."

"Hey, boo. What's up?"

"Nothin', chile. Men, girl."

"Men? Oh, hell no," she said. "I know the playette can't be complaining about men."

"Who said I was complaining?" I snapped.

"Your nasty-ass attitude."

"Well . . ." I decided to just spill it. I had to talk to somebody. "Taj was over here, and I was talking to Roger on the phone."

"He caught you?"

"Yeah, girl," I admitted.

"Then yo' ass was dead wrong."

"Dead wrong? I'm not married to him!"

"And you won't be getting married doing dumb shit."

"Dumb shit?"

"Dumb shit," she said. "Stupid moves."

"So what should I do?"

"Apologize."

"Oh, hell no! He wanna play tough, two can play at that game."

"Yeah? Well, you do that and see how far that gets you. And when you got another bitch sneaking in during your in-between time of playing a game, take your beating like a champ."

"I really didn't call you for this," I insisted.

"Yeah, you did. You knew what you were going to get when you called here. That's why you called me, as opposed to Lee or Angie. You knew they would pacify yo' ass, and you needed to be knocked in the head with the truth."

"Bye, Shannon."

"Love ya, girl, but I gotta go anyway. I'm 'bout to get my swerve on!"

Fuck it. I called Taj at his apartment, and his voice mail came on. "Hey, Taj. Vera. Hope all is well. Call me when you get a chance."

Then I slammed the pillow over my head and felt stupid. *Fuck him. I think it's some ice cream in the refrigerator.*

In between the first swirl of caramel and chocolate chunk, the phone rang. I peeped the caller ID and saw it was Taj. I didn't answer the phone.

"Hey, Vera," he said into the answering machine. "Figures you wouldn't answer the phone. I'm sure I peeped your card, but anyway, when you're done—"

I snatched the phone off the receiver. "You didn't peep no card of mine."

"Hello?"

"You heard me," I said, tight-lipped.

"Hey, baby!"

"Don't 'hey, baby' me!"

"Damn, lots of attitude. Do I suspect a problem?"

"No, no problem. No problem at all. As a matter fact, I have to get up and go to the shop right about now."

"It's seven o'clock in the morning."

"It sure is. Great answer. *Ciao, bella.*" I hung up on the mu'fucka!

Now, when the morning's rush came into the shop, the old ladies, the gossip mouths, and some of Aunt Cookie's girlfriends, the last thing I needed was to hear how Aunt Cookie was creeping. It almost made me sick. How the hell was she getting extra dick when I hadn't had any in three days, not to mention she lives with my Uncle Boy?

And to make matters worse, Aunt Cookie's girlfriend Ms. Janet told me that somebody needed to talk to Uncle Boy, 'cause all he seemed to be doing was crying and explaining to anybody who would listen that Gladys Knight had a midnight train for him to catch, and as soon as daybreak hit, he planned to be on the next thing smokin'. This shit couldn't have come at a worse time.

Immediately, I called Uncle Boy and whispered into the phone in an effort to keep the shop out of my business. "Don't cry, Uncle Boy. Don't leave. Don't do that."

"Uncle Boy, don't do that? Naw, you misunderstandin' yo' Uncle Boy. I'm tired of yo' Aunt Cookie."

"Uncle Boy, Aunt Cookie loves you and you know that."

"Well, if lovin' me is wrong, then goddamnit, don't be right."

"Uncle Boy, you been drinkin'?"

"Naw, baby," he said with a slur. "I been caught up."

"Caught up in what?"

"A one-night love affair!"

I couldn't take it anymore, so I made a few phone calls, one to Shannon's mother and the other to Lee's mother, who in turn, informed me that they left Aunt Cookie on Utica at Ms. Carol's house, hosting an all-night card party, and if I wanted to catch the last game, I needed to hurry.

I hung up the phone and asked DeAndre to please finish my client's hair while I went to see about Aunt Cookie.

When I arrived at Ms.Carol's, I could hear Chaka Khan's "Whatcha Gonna Do for Me" blasting down the hallway. I knocked on the door and Ms. Carol yelled, "It cost two dollars to get up in here!"

"Ms. Carol, I just came to see my Aunt Cookie."

"That's what they all say, and the next thing I know, they got a hand goin'. Cough it up, honey chile!"

"I got the two dollars!" Aunt Cookie yelled from behind the door.

Aunt Cookie, Ms. Carol, and two other women all had men counterparts sitting around the small card table. None of them seemed to mind that I was there and knew for a fact that each of them, including Ms Carol, had their own live-in boyfriends.

So they sat with their sister-girl, young-looking forty-nine- and fifty-year-old faces, with hot red and mellow pink lipstick on, big wigs, and hoop earrings, all the while chewing gum and taking turns slamming down cards and yelling, "Six, no uptown!"

Aunt Cookie had on a tight catsuit with her stomach poked out just a little. Her makeup was flawless, and her blue eyeshadow hadn't missed a beat. She had one of the biggest asses in Brooklyn, which always got attention, and she was workin' it as she walked around the room introducing me as Babygirl.

"Whatcha workin' wit', Babygirl?" Aunt Cookie asked, sounding slightly drunk and making googly eyes at Earl Gatling.

"I'm workin' with a drunk-ass old man crying on my phone, talking about how he taking a midnight train to Georgia!"

"Who? Boy?"

"Who else?"

"Hell, Boy ain't from Georgia, his ass from Uptown."

"Whatever," I said, "but word on the street is that you over here," I said, pointing to Earl Gatling, "screwing around with what's-his-name."

"Oh, wait a minute, Babygirl. Step off now. This is grown folk bidness."

"Aunt Cookie, you need to get home!"

"I will. Earl just stopped by to see me. He be gone in the morning, because his wife be back in town."

"His wife?"

"Yeah, baby. You know how I do it. Aunt Cookie ain't stupid now. Ain't nobody like Boy, and if I'ma creep, then the next nigga got to have as much to lose. Now, you go 'head to the shop, and I'll meet you there. Let Aunt Cookie take care of Uncle Boy, 'cause what I can do, you can't handle." She winked her eye, threw her hips to the side, and strutted her stuff.

Marvin Gaye was banging the hell outta the high note of "Let's Get It On" as I was leaving.

"What the hell?" DeAndre was saying as I walked in the shop, frowning his nose up. "You smell like Black Love incense. You been hittin' a joint?"

"Please, DeAndre."

"Then what's your problem?" Shannon asked, untangling her double strand twist.

"Aunt Cookie cheating on Uncle Boy."

"That's why you smell like blue lights and wooden beads?"

"Whatever. But can you believe that Aunt Cookie is cheating on Uncle Boy, and she think the shit is all good?"

"What's the problem?"

"She lives with Uncle Boy, and she's cheating with a married man. She, of all people, has no business cheating!"

"Oh, no you didn't, diva!" DeAndre said. "What about yo' sugar daddy?"

Sugar daddy? Oh, hell. I practically forgot about Roger, but I wouldn't let them know that. "But still, my Aunt Cookie and my Uncle Boy?"

"Gettin' they groove on!" DeAndre said.

"Hey-hey now!" Aunt Cookie said, coming in, throwing her hips around and having the nerve to be glowing! "Show me whatcha workin' wit'!" she said to everybody in the shop. "How y'all?"

All the women in the shop were making plans to go to dinner, a church function, or to see a man, and they seemed to be having a good time getting themselves hooked up. All the overhead dryers were filled, and the three weave operators had been sewing on hair for over an hour. The manicurist seemed to be making mad loot, 'cause there were already two women with their nails drying, one woman in the chair, and another one with her feet soaking for a pedicure.

Fifty Cent's "Get Rich or Die Trying" was banging in the background, leading nobody to notice how Rowanda came in well dressed, pretending to be clean. I ignored the hell outta her. I was embarrassed, and if it weren't for the memory of the ass-beatin' I got from Aunt Cookie when I spit in Rowanda's face, I would've done it again.

"Hey, Cookie!" Rowanda said.

"Hey, chile! What you doin' here?"

"Yesterday was my birthday."

"That's beautiful, baby. Happy birthday," Aunt Cookie said.

"Well, I don't have two dollars!" I said, trying to shut Rowanda down before she even got to the part where she needed two dollars for something to eat, or two dollars for something to drink, or to get to a job, or any other shit that the typical fiend would create.

"She ain't asked you fo' two dollars!" Aunt Cookie snapped. "Yesterday was your mother's birthday. Show some respect."

"My mother? Please." Then I rolled my eyes and proceeded with handling my client's hair.

"I ain't come for no trouble," Rowanda said. "I just was wonderin' if you would do my hair. See, I got money. I got a whole ten dollars."

"Well, the ten dollar doobie shop is down the street and around the corner."

Aunt Cookie shot me the evil eye. "Step to the side for a minute, Vera," Aunt Cookie said in a demanding tone.

"What is it?" I snapped.

"Now, look. That there is yo' mama. Treat her nice for once. She trying, Vera."

"Be nice? Be nice? That chickenhead put me in a drawstring garbage bag and placed me on the street like overnight trash!"

"You gonna have to get over that."

"Really? Well, until I do, she won't get her hair done up in here."

"Hey, baby," Taj said, walking into the midst of commotion. Now, personally, this mu'fucka had a lot of nerve, but I was relieved as hell to see him.

"Where did you come from? Your hair appointment is not until tomorrow." *Now, take that, put it in yo' pipe and smoke it! Teach yo' ass not to call me for three days.*

He shot my ass such a look that I instantly took it down, but I still ignored the hell outta Aunt Cookie and Rowanda.

"Taj," Aunt Cookie said, "speak with Vera! She acting like she don't have no Christianity!"

"What's up, baby?" he had the audacity to say, sounding as if something was wrong with me.

Well, wasn't a damn thing wrong with me! Didn't nobody in there know what it was like to have a dopefiend for a mother. Nobody knew what it was like to wanna eat but have to wait until everybody had their dope. Nobody knew! And here Taj came, who hadn't called me in three days, and he thought that I should what, pour my heart out to his ass? Hell, no. Not Vera.

"Ain't shit up!" I said, taking the cape off my client and winking my eye to let her know she looked good. "But I'm not doing Rowanda's hair. Understand?"

I felt my knees about to break, but there was no way I would let any one of these mu'fuckas see me cry. I cleared my throat, wrote out my ticket for my client to pay the cashier, and then I planned to keep on steppin'.

Instead, Taj handed the cashier the ticket and stepped into my personal space. I could feel the cool peppermint on his breath.

"Let's talk," he said.

Reluctantly, I stepped to the back of the shop, where my small office was. I practically fell down in my oversized brown leather chair, placed my head on my desk and began to cry. How could Rowanda come in here and humiliate me? And how could Aunt Cookie let her? Why was it that I had to accept Rowanda? I hated the bitch! I hated the sound of her voice, and the way she reminded me of broken elevators, lion claw tubs, and blood.

"Look, baby," Taj said, "ease up a little bit. Cut Rowanda some slack."

"Cut Rowanda some slack? What about cutting me some slack?" I said, with snot dripping.

At this point, I didn't care what he thought. Hell, he wasn't my man. I was my own man. I ain't need him for shit!

"You got a lot of fuckin' nerve, Mister Yuppie-ass emergency room doctor! What do you know about being born in hell? You never came from a crackfiend's pussy. You've never seen dope being slowly released from a bloody needle and yo' grandma moanin' about how it feel good, and all the while you wondering if she shootin' up the rent money or the food stamps! You know what it's like to starve, Taj? I didn't think so!" I opened my office door and said, "Get the fuck out!"

Taj turned around and grabbed me by my forearm. "Vera, throwing me out is no issue. I'm a cocky-ass black man from Newark, with a doctorate degree in medicine. I've been thrown out by the best of 'em, but you have to live with you. You must stop all of this self-defeating madness or else you will be strung out on a damn nervous breakdown.

"Now, I'm here because you need me here. I'm already in your heart, so you can stop faking like throwing me out is easy. When you're ready to stop throwing a tantrum, we'll talk." And he slammed the door behind him.

I leaned against the wall and slowly slid down to the floor, feeling as if my chest would cave in. I wanted desperately to run after Taj and beg him to come back, but my pride wouldn't let me. Instead, I pulled my knees up to my chest, tilted my head down, and cried. I cried so much that when I lifted my head up, my vision was blurry. I wiped my eyes, placed my head back down, and while the whistle of the breeze came through the window, thoughts of Rowanda raced through my mind.

I thought that at some point I would be able to come back and finish working in the shop, but when I looked around, it seemed that everyone had left. At least five hours had gone by and I hadn't even noticed.

The darkness was comforting and cool. The window was cracked just a little, and I could hear the whistle of the cold breeze. The dampness of the wind reminded me of winter in the projects, and of the time when the lights were shut off and there were no candles to burn.

I was seven years old and petrified of the dark. "I'm scared, Rowanda," I said into the ear of the darkness. "I'm scared." Nobody answered, but I could see Rowanda searching for a match, while I crossed my small seven-year-old legs and sat around the stove, wanting desperately to feel the heat.

Rowanda wore high heels and a blond wig. She snuck out at night and nobody ever noticed. Grandma never cared. Rowanda would say how she always met a john and that I ain't have to worry as long as she had the block locked.

"What you scared of, girl? I'm here." And she was. Even when her pimp stomped her in the face for not having all of his money, she still made sure I had something to eat. Getting stomped was just a chance she had to take.

Rowanda found a match, and she reached and placed her head inside the stove. The gas fumes were rising, and when she placed the small fire on the pilot, she never really screamed when her face caught fire. She barely made a noise as the skin curled off, and even when the kids teased her and said that she looked like Scarface, she still hustled the block. She never even worried about how half of her beauty was left burning on the pilot of the gas stove.

I fumbled along the wall for the light switch, because I couldn't take my thoughts anymore. When I walked into the shop, I saw Taj sleeping in my station chair. I walked over to him and kissed him on his forehead.

"I'm sorry, Taj."

He swiveled the chair around and grabbed me by my waist. "You need to stop this tough-girl routine. You're chasing everybody away."

"I don't mean to chase everybody away, but—"

"But what? Don't you know that you're worth loving? Trust me, otherwise I wouldn't be here. What are you so scared of?"

"Everything," I found myself admitting. "Of dopefiends, lion claw tubs, men with silver belt buckles."

"Why?"

"Because that's all that I see."

"Then see me. I'm here."

"Why?"

"Baby, I'm in love with you. But I'm not the type to pamper a little girl. I want a woman. And if you have to cry, baby, it's all good, but you have to be a woman about the situation no matter what. That sad, deprived little girl routine has to end. Plus, I think you're kinda cute wit' your stubborn ass."

"Stubborn?"

"Mad crazy stubborn," he said, giving me a peck across the lips.

"And you love every bit of it."

"Too much of it."

"Taj, I'm sorry about Roger and the other day."

"Yeah?" he said with a smirk.

"Yeah, I'm really sorry."

"Good, 'cause those three days without you were hell."

"Um, well, I was fine. No sweat. Those three days were a breeze."

He tilted his head and looked at me out the corner of his eye. "Yeah? The three days were a breeze? And you could breathe without me? You weren't all *Waiting to Exhale* on the phone with the girlfriends, doggin' me out?"

"Could I breathe? Please, what you think? And on the phone with the girlfriends? My girlfriends and I, we don't even talk like that."

"Yeah, right."

"Yeah, right? Well, could you breathe?"

"No."

"Oh."

Step Four

"If that ain't 'bout the corniest shit that I have ever heard! He need you to breathe. What he gonna do if you go outta town? Die? His ass ain't Eddie Murphy. Y'all been watching too much TV!" Shannon said as she tried to squeeze her size sixteen into a pair of size twelve jeans.

"I'm losing weight, girl. Can't you tell?" she said.

"I can tell you fuckin' up those jeans!"

"Whatever. Get to the real shit. You trying to slip up on me?"

"Excuse me?"

"Excuse me? You heard me. You trying to fall in love on me, Miss Vera? Miss 'A big dick is just a big dick.'"

"Taj is different."

"And how is that? He got a little dick?"

"Oh, you think yo' ass is funny! For your information, he got a Mandingo, Zulu warrior, West African dick!"

"What, he got one of those Kunta Kinte dicks?"

"Big and strong, like dynamite!"

"Mm-hmm, and it got yo' ass sewed the hell up!"

"All right, I'll admit I'm feeling him a little bit, but I'm not ready to commit."

"Take yo' time, girlfriend. One thing about love, its ass is persistent."

"Love? Chile, please! I ain't hardly in love."

"Yeah, that's the same thing Lee said."

Lee? I know this heifer didn't just compare me to Lee. Lee was a whole 'nother ball game, but nevertheless, she was our girl, and the shit that her man pulled on her was enough to make us wanna kick his ass.

Lee had waltzed in the shop on Valentine's Day with a gorgeous black tree, also known as James. I couldn't help but stare, because I was shocked as shit. As a matter of fact, the entire shop was shocked. Here was the black Laura Ingalls, with Tyson on her arm. Hmph! Well, when Aunt Cookie saw these two, she almost died, and if it wasn't for her being ashamed, I do believe that she would've cussed the black tree out.

"What is your problem, Cookie Turner?"

"Nothing," she snapped. "I just gotta go."

"Why are you going out the back door?"

She placed her hands on her hips and said, "Didn't you just see what the dog drug in? You'll never have me be a part of that."

At worse, I figured the man was married to one of Aunt Cookie's girlfriends' daughters or something.

"Is he married, Lee?" I called her to the back and asked.

"No, he isn't married. Not yet anyway," she said, laughing and wagging her ring finger.

"Just be careful."

"Girl, please," she said, waving me off and blowing kisses at him from my office door. "I got this."

And what she got was a fine mu'fuckin' dog. Now, he was fine. Let me repeat that: he was extremely fine. Black as a coal mine, with a body that wore the essence of Africa. His eyes were a deep dark brown, and his eyelashes seemed to be the crowning of his strong, chiseled face. He spoke as if he had invented confidence, and all of this man stood about six foot three. And when he walked, Jesus! When he walked, he seemed to float above the floor, and he would slither in with his Versace double-breasted suit and his lips would glide as he said hello. Therefore, as you can imagine, when he walked in the shop, the entire operation shut the fuck down.

There was very little attention being paid to the fact that he was slowly taking control. When he told Lee that she needed to lose weight, she thought the shit was great. When he told her that she needed to carry Ucchi instead of Gucci, she thought he was considerate. But what did it was when the nigga called me on the phone, with Angie and Shannon on the three-way, telling us that we needed to practice "minding our business," because the tongue was a serpent, and the way he saw it, Eddie Murphy had a point and Oum FuFu needed to stay the hell away from the girlfriend crew!

Now, that straight set the shit off. After he hung up on us, Shannon called Angie and me back, and we had our own conference call, better known as the get-'im-girl session. That's when we decided it was on like popcorn!

"All right," I said, while lying on the bed. "I'll make Roger think he's getting some ass so I can get some background information."

"Good," Angie said, "and I'll try and screw the li'l twenty-two-year-old security guard downtown at the Prudential Building."

"What?"

"Girl, you got to see him. He got an ass like butta!" she screeched.

"What does that have to do with Lee?"

"Nothing. I just figured since we were discussing men in law enforcement that I would throw that out there."

Anyway, Angie screwing the li'l security guard did nothing for Lee, and me making Roger think he and I would always be together didn't do shit either. Instead, it aggravated the situation between Roger and me, and as the saying goes, desperate times call for desperate measures. So, I had to swallow my pride and beg the truth out of Aunt Cookie.

All she said was, "You, Angie, and Shannon need to meet me at the church for revival tonight." So, we obeyed and went dragging along.

When we arrived at church, we slid in the last pew on the left side, all the way in the back, near the section where most people eat and go to sleep.

When the choir started singing, I turned to Angie and gave her explicit instructions. "If you get in here and start beatin' that tambourine and hollerin' out in tongue, I'ma slap you!"

"You have officially lost your mind," she said. "Now, mess with me and I'll make the old ladies come back here and lay hands on you."

Before I could respond, out walks the pastor dressed in a purple robe with "The Blood of

Jesus" written across his chest. Oh my God! I had to do a double take, because there was Lee's man, armed with a Bible, and his first lady sittin' and grinnin' in the third row. Needless to say, church was over for us. Now we had to figure out a way to break the news to Lee. Me, I figured just let the bitch have it straight out, but nooo. Shannon and Angie insisted that we hold onto the information until they felt Lee was strong enough to handle it. They insisted that she was too fragile.

"Fragile?" I asked.

"Fragile," Shannon and Angie said simultaneously.

"Her ass ain't fragile. She just stupid!"

And since then, those two had been walking around Lee on eggshells, as if she was Princess Di or some shit, but I didn't think so. The way I figured, revenge is sweet, but a divafied scorn is a bitch.

So, I squatted and waited patiently on our monthly fake-ass book club meeting, because it was more like girlfriends' gossip hour. I made sure that this session was at Shannon's house. After all, I couldn't take the chance of Miz Thing reverting back to the playground days at Prospect Park and leaving tear stains on my three-hundred-dollar silk embroidered pillows.

I figured since Shannon had a red Coach leather sofa with the pillows to match, what better place to lay it on the line?

Angie and Lee walked in Shannon's front door together, laughing and acting giddy.

"Where are you two coming from?" I asked.

"Short Hills Mall," Angie said.

"Correction," Lee said. "The Mall of Short Hills. I picked James up a leather jacket from Wilson's Leather."

Instantly, I shot Angie the evil eye. "Don't be playing her like that!" I said, tight-lipped.

"I tried to tell her not to buy it, but she insisted."

"Yeah, right!"

An hour into Angie and Shannon's lollygagging and making small talk about the weather, work, and the new Louie V. Sharon Stone bag, I absolutely couldn't take it anymore. I slammed both my elbows on Shannon's wicker trunk and said, "Look, don't spend any more money on that mu'fuckin' James. That mu'fucka is a damn snake! He's married!"

"And a pastor at Holy Rock Tabernacle," Angie interjected.

"What!" Lee exclaimed. "What are they talking about? Shannon, what are they saying?"

Oh, no this bitch didn't! *What are they saying, Shannon?* Like she was trying for a Daytime Emmy in melodrama. "Bitch, this ain't the *Young and the Restless*. You heard what I said!"

"It's not as bad as it may seem," Shannon said, lying her ass off.

"That so-'n-so ain't even a good piece of shit!" I insisted, waiving my hands in the air. "That nigga is the pimp of the pulpit, and it turns out you his bottom bitch!"

"Who the fuck are you?" Shannon asked sarcastically.

"Snoop Dog, Ice-T and shit? We don't need yo' pimped-out version of this. Take that shit down now. That's enough! We need to discuss what we're going to do about the man who thinks he can dis and dismiss one of the divafied Queens. Oh, no. I don't think so!"

"Well, I tell y'all what," Lee said, while grabbing her jacket and car keys. "Jealousy will get you all nowhere." Then she rolled her eyes and held her arm up as if she were saying, "Tell it to the hand!"

As soon as the bitch did that, I started hearing sirens and shit, bells and whistles going off and screaming, "Dumb bitch alert!"

"I know," I turned to Lee and said, "that you don't think I'm jealous of you 'cause you finally found a man that can tolerate, feed, and fuck yo' fat ass?"

"Oh, no you didn't!" Lee rolled her eyes and said, "Everybody's coochie can't tolerate a thousand dicks at once, ho."

"Ho? You the trick bein' played by a goddamn televangelist!"

"Oh, no you didn't go there!" she screamed.

"Yes, I did!"

See, let me tell y'all somethin'. The only reason I could stand her was because she was like a pain-in-the-ass sister, and we'd been friends since we were eight. Otherwise, I woulda cold-cocked her stank ass the minute she stood up in my face and started runnin' her mouth.

I turned to her and said, "Here we are, looking out for you, and you talkin' major shit."

"First of all, Miz Thang, y'all got issues with men, so can't none of y'all open your mouth to tell me nothin' about my man."

"Lee," Shannon said, still trying to be calm, "you really need to be quiet, because we love you and would never tell you anything that would hurt you."

"Shannon," I turned to her and said, "why are you trying to baby this ho? Lee is a big girl. If she wanna be the black version of Joann Buttafuoco, sit back, and bask in the essence of getting dogged, then by all means, let the bitch! 'Cause you know me, and my sympathy goes two places, to the starving kids in Ethiopia, and to Luther when he gains weight. That's right, that's the extent of it, so I don't feel sorry for Lee."

I turned to Lee and said, "If you like it, I'm in love wit' it."

"That ain't right, Vera," Angie chimed in.

"You know Luther sick. He can't help his situation. Somebody gonna fuck you up for that one. You need to apologize."

Oh, now they wanted to gang up on a sista. "Shut up, Angela! Luther ain't even here. You need to be worried about dumb-dumb over there."

"Call me out my name again," Lee said, dropping her things on the floor.

I just looked at the heifer, 'cause it's amazing what a good piece of dick will do to ya. This heifer ain't never won a fight in her life, and now she wanted to fight me!

"Excuse you?" I said, looking her up and down. "You wanna do something? If you don't, sit yo' ass down."

"Lee, you are way outta line!" Shannon said, jumping in between us.

"I can't believe this shit," Angie said. "Maybe I need to go back to Alabama, 'cause y'all New

York bitches are crazy. Now, Lee," Angie said with a Southern twang, "I understand that you love James. I respect that. But the nigga is a pastor, and he's dogging you. Nobody here is jealous. We're just being honest with you."

"I got yo' honest," Lee said, pointing around the room.

"You, you, and you need to mind your business, ya fake-ass Oprah and Gail King wannabes!" She picked up her stuff and left our dumb asses sittin' there.

It had been three weeks since I had heard from the ho, with the exception of the chain letter e-mails she'd been sending me. But, as sure as my name is Vera, I was certain that her day would come. I just didn't think it would be this soon.

I was in the middle of gettin' my groove on and Shannon called. I was breathing heavy, sweatin' and shit. Taj was hittin' that spot, and right at the point where all my juices were about to explode, Shannon yelled into the answering machine for me to pick up the phone! Goddamn it! But she said that it was an emergency.

"What, Shannon?" *Stay right there*, I said to Taj with my eyes, trying to get him not to move. "Shannon, what do you want? I'm busy!"

"Bitch! You done had more than enough dick to last you two or three lifetimes. You shoulda done made yo' money, ho. So sit up, roll over, or whatever you got to do, but you gonna have to hear this one."

"What?"

"Don't you know that Lee saw the nigga out with his wife, and when Lee confronted him, he looked at her like she was crazy and acted as if he had never seen her before? Talking about, 'Do I know you?' I told Lee she shoulda said, 'Nigga, yo' goddamn mouth know my pussy, ya fake-ass, Jello-pop-eatin' mu'fucka!"

"Well, what she do?"

"She started crying and shit. Talking about, 'James, how could you? How could you?'"

"And what the wife do?"

"She lost her damn mind! Started actin' a fool, jumpin' up and down, telling Lee that she was gonna fuck her up. This trick performed! You hear me? But since Lee was by herself, she just walked away crying and shit."

"She did what? She was gonna fight me, but she walk away from James and his wife? Lee's ass is a punk! Plus, I don't know what you telling me for. I don't feel sorry for the bitch, not one bit. We told Lee that the man was married, and she insisted that she didn't believe us, so she got what she had coming to her. Na'mean? Hell, I ain't mad. If she insist on being played, then by all means, 'cause see, if I was Lee, me and my Aunt Cookie woulda invited the bitch for a showdown and I woulda shot her ass!"

Taj looked at me in disbelief. I rolled my eyes and kept my conversation movin'. "Anyway, boo, do you," I said, "because I'm not gettin' involved. The dumb bitch won't make a liar outta me no more. Had me use my resources and for what? Nah, that's yo' girl. You handle that."

Shannon sat on the phone for a minute and she didn't say anything, but I heard her breathing, so I knew she was still on the phone.

"Hello," I said.

First silence, then the breathing stopped, and then there was a dial tone. So fuck it, I thought, and I continued with my don't-stop, get it—get it orgasm, and kept it movin'.

Taj stayed with me until it was time for him to work the night shift. After he left, I turned over and looked at the phone, feeling guilty about my conversation with Shannon. I knew she had to be pissed with me if she hadn't called back yet. I picked up the phone and dialed her number.

"Hey, Shannon." I said, eating major crow.

"Yeah."

"Wassup?" I said reluctantly. "Y'all wanna roll?"

"Hell, yeah!"

"When?"

"First thing in the morning. And be dressed for church."

"A'ight. Come through and get me. I'll be ready."

"Good thing you called back, bitch! I was just buying time, tryin' to wait for boyfriend to go for his night shift, and then I was comin' over to wreck shop! Love ya." And she hung up.

Later that night, Shannon and Lee called me on the three-way, and according to my calculations, Lee cried all night. I couldn't take it, so I put the phone down and started cleaning my house. Every time I went back to the phone to see if they were still talking, I heard a lot of snot blowing and Lee crying, "Why? Why? Why?"

Six a.m. couldn't get there fast enough. When the alarm clock went off, I was happy as hell. Roger called saying that he wanted to come by, but I told him that I needed to go to church.

He started breathing heavy and sounding scared. "Does this mean you don't want anything to do with me?"

"What?"

"Does this mean that, you know, you think adultery is wrong?"

"What you think?" I hung up. I had no time for the bullshit, and Roger seemed to be going too far to the left. I had a preacher to teach, so I had no time for the captain of the NYPD trying to act guilty on me.

After waiting five minutes for Shannon to arrive, I called her. "What's taking you so long?"

"I'm putting on my one-piece!" And she hung up.

I gave myself one last overview before I stepped outside, and believe me, to say that I looked good as hell would be an understatement. My black Chanel dress with the mink collar had me looking quite exquisite. If I didn't know better, I would swear that I resembled an hourglass, with an extra fifteen minutes on the side!

Finally, the crew rolled up, and I could hear the *Shaft* music playing in my mind as I stepped in Shannon's gold 745i.

"Who the hell said Charlie's Angels had to always be white?" Angie said, as she slapped me five on the black hand side.

Lee had the nerve to still be crying. "Damn, Lee, you still crying?" I said. "You been gettin' dogged long enough to be a big girl about the shit by now! Jesus!"

"Shut up!" Shannon said. "Y'all just started speaking again, so be quiet."

I checked the car over, peeped our gear, and saw we were looking fierce. Angie was decked from head to toe in her off-white suede dress. The top part crossed over the breast and tied on the side. Shannon's dress had about five crisscrosses in the back and an asymmetrical dip in the front. Lee wore a light blue wool, fox fur trimmed two-piece suit. The sky blue hat she wore had a large brim and a small black veil in the front. The mere fact that the first lady would see us looking so sharp should be enough to let her know that she would be beaten hands down.

The first person we saw when we got to the church door was Aunt Cookie. She was the head usher, and of all Sundays, she would be at the door.

"Don't start no mess, Babygirl. This is the sanctuary. Move it to the parking lot," she said, handing me a program.

The usher standing in the front of the church tried to get us to sit all the way on the left side of the church, in the back where nobody could see us. We ignored her and sat in the center aisle, third row, directly behind the mother's bench, not caring about the looks we got for sitting in somebody's space. We had to be sure that Pastor James knew exactly who was in the house.

At first there was some singing, then the standing for the choir, and then the sermon was to begin. Mr. Big Stuff walked to the front of the altar, and then he paraded around like he was the Holy Ghost fire. He huffed his shoulders, cleared his throat, and he just about choked when he spotted us sitting in the third row.

It wasn't time to blow up his spot just yet, so to get it goin', I yelled out, "Tell it, Pastor! Fix it!"

He cleared his throat. "Brothas and sistas, I'm here to tell you today that the devil is a liar and the tongue is a serpent."

"Amen!" I said, tapping Angie on the knee so she could hit the tambourine. "Amen!"

"Jesus said that a man must cleave unto his wife, for they are one. And so, we must honor our wives and stop the backbiting and the backsliding."

"Amen!" *Ching-ching*! went the tambourine.

"And let he without sin cast the first stone!"

I jumped up and said, and trust me this was difficult, especially being in church and not being able to cuss, "Pastor James, you are about as sanctified as horse manure. You got cow slop beat! And if you think that your religion only applies on the weekend, you are certifiably twisted."

"'Cause it ain't all good." Lee gathered the courage to say, "It ain't all good in the good Lord's neighborhood, when you cheating and scheming. You ain't Mr. Clean, Pastor James!"

"I rebuke you, Satan!" Pastor James insisted like he was desperate and lost for words. "I rebuke you!"

"You can't rebuke nobody. The two chickens on Noah's boat got more religion than you! You got about as much religion as a cow, and you goin' to hell, 'cause you know better! He goin' to hell, Mrs. First Lady, 'cause he ain't doing right. And when he was laying in my bed the other night, he was cleaving all right, but it wasn't to you!"

"Oh, hell naw!" the first lady hollered. She stood up, looking just like a sanctified Laura Hayes, removed her hat, slid off her shoes, and invited Lee to get it goin'.

"Ain't nothin' but a word!" the first lady said, with the deaconesses by her side, standing like Nation of Islam soldiers. "What? What? Y'all wanna do somethin'? Somebody got a beef?"

Holy shit! I couldn't believe this! Talk about ghettofied saints. Now, had I known I would be fightin' in church, I would've placed my nunchucks in my bag, not to mention left my black leather stilettos at home!

Aunt Cookie shot me a look, but hell, I woulda never guessed that the first lady would come out the side of her neck like that! Now, I'm 'bout to go to hell for fightin' the preacher's wife and the sanctified crew.

"You couldn't get no baller bitch?" I said to Lee. "Somebody we could just shoot and keep it movin'? Now I got to fight the Virgin Mary and shit! Goddamnit!"

The first lady was hopping around, and Pastor James was demanding that we leave. I kept making eye contact with Aunt Cookie, looking for a way out, or for her to say something. All she said was, "Long as don't nobody touch you, we straight. But if the heifer jump over the bench, we gonna throw!"

"You about dumb as he is!" Lee said, continuing to talk shit, never mind that we were outnumbered. "You know what? Bump dis. We in the Lord's house."

"That's right," Pastor James intercepted.

"So, I tell you what," Lee continued, sounding like Shay-Shay from the thirty-fifth floor of the projects. "Bring it outside!"

Now, I knew damn well that this bitch didn't just say "Bring it outside." I looked at Shannon, and if looks could kill, this bitch would be buried.

"That heifer can't fight long enough to save her own life," I mumbled to Shannon. "And, now she done invited somebody for a war, and in the church's parking lot? Oh, hell no. Soon as we get outside, fuck the pastor's wife. I'ma kick Lee's ass!"

Lee snapped her fingers and said, "Let's go!" And the heifer went walking out the door.

You could tell that Lee didn't have any boxing skills, 'cause she turned her back on the bitch. Guess who had to walk out backward, hunchin' their shoulders and talking shit? You got it: Angie, Shannon, and me. I was fuming!

"This what we gonna do," Lee instructed us as we walked out the door with half of the church, including the first lady, following us. "Vera, you gonna gut-punch her ass. Shannon, you grab her by the hair and pull her down to the ground, and Angie, you gonna stomp her."

"And what you gonna do, bitch?" I asked.

"I'ma make sure don't nobody get hurt!"

Holy shit! I knew it. Here we were again, taking up for Lee like we used to do when the girls from down the block used to fuck with her in Prospect Park. Lee couldn't fight, but she always seemed to end up in the midst of some shit.

Pastor James came running outside and pushing the first lady back as she went to take a swing at Lee. "Y'all, please," he begged. "I understand, lawd Jesus. You done made yo' point. Come on and go home. I'm beggin' ya, please."

"Naw!" Lee said, jumping up and down like she was going to do something. "Naw, bring it! Bring it! I betcha know me now!"

"I'ma fuck Lee up!" I said to Shannon.

"She 'bout to get it!"

"Lee," Shannon said, "you done proved your point. Shut the fuck up and let's go! You gonna fuck around here and get yo' ass beat, and I got a date tonight, so I ain't playin' witcha like that."

"All right," Lee said as if she were doing us a favor. "No problem, but the next time, Miz First Lady, you gonna wear yo' words! Come on, girls. Let's blow this joint!"

As we turned to leave, we heard someone calling our names. "Vera, Shannon, Lee, and Angie!" Aunt Cookie said, running over toward Shannon's car. "If it wasn't for a li'l bit, I would break each and every one of y'all asses! Don't you ever come up to my church and start no shit in the sanctuary. You was s'posed to catch the bitch on the way to her ride and sneak her ass, not put the pastor on Front Street in the midst of the congregation. Y'all have lost yo' minds! Now, I got to go and try to make things right, 'cause you four don't know how to play yo' cards!

"And, Lee, don't you ever mess with another married man if you can't deal. Now, take y'all asses home, 'fore I straight wreck shop out this piece!"

When we got in Shannon's car, I advised Lee that it would be in her best interest to never speak to me again in life, and if she couldn't manage that, then to at least give me a week, because I'd had enough of her dumb ass to last me a lifetime.

Step Five

"Get the door. What are you waiting on?" Taj said as he placed a pot of grits on the stove. He had no shirt on, and he refused to grab my housecoat for me, even after I told him that it was Roger at the door.

"Roger who?" he said with a smirk. "Roger couldn't possibly be my problem." And he was right; he was mine.

"But let me tell you this," Taj said, finally throwing me my housecoat. "You better tell ole boy that I ain't the one, and you better understand that as well, 'cause I will leave yo' ass right here!"

"But, Taj, I didn't even do anything."

"Can it, Vera. You're not stupid. Now, you play me if you want to. Try me and see how it really feels to be alone."

"Roger," I said, cracking the door halfway. "It's eight o'clock in the morning. What are you doing here?"

"What?"

"Roger, look, this has to stop. You're going too far. Let's just end this while we can still be civilized."

"Civilized? What? You trying to play games with me? Why haven't you answered the phone? I called all last night and no answer. You might think you slick, but I saw ole boy come in your house last night. Who was he?"

"What? You been watching me? Are you crazy?"

"Crazy? No. Pissed off? Yes. Plus, this is a high crime area."

"A high crime area? This conversation is finished!"

"Finished?"

"Yes. Done. Over with."

"All right, all right. I understand that you're pissed. Just calm down. I was concerned. How about lunch later today?"

"Lunch?"

"Vera, we gotta talk, and I won't take no for an answer. One o'clock at One Fish, Two Fish. Be there." Then he jumped in his undercover police car, started the sirens to blaring, and took off.

When I walked back into the house, Taj slapped me on the ass as he walked out the door.

"Where are you going?"

"The hospital paged me. It's an emergency."

"An emergency?"

"Yes, an emergency. Now, I started to get straight ghetto, come outside on the stoop, and handle some shit, but I didn't. Only because you needed to put him in his place. But the next time—and trust me, this is not a threat; it's a promise—I will step to his ass. Don't fuckin' play me, because where I come from, men get killed for less than that. Therefore, if you go to lunch wit' ole boy today, don't ask no questions on why you're alone."

"Why do you keep threatening me?"

"That's not a threat. That's a promise. Now, be slick and dumb if you want to." He walked over, kissed me on the side of my neck, and then he left.

I looked out the living room window and watched him get in his Escalade and leave. I was bored as hell. I had closed the shop today, because it was a Monday and I needed a day off, but shit, I was not used to this. I had to do something.

Damn, believe me when I tell you that I tried so hard to behave myself, and I knew I was dead wrong, but One Fish, Two Fish was tight as hell, hardly any elbow room. It wasn't hard for me to spot Roger and his wife having a luncheon rendezvous. This confirmed it for me: Roger was crazy. If he thought he was gonna get this one off, he had another thing comin'.

I purposely asked to sit at the table next to Captain and Mrs. Roger Sims. I spoke to both of them as I sat down and complimented his wife on how beautiful she looked. In my mind, I was daring the bitch to get nasty, and I was praying that she recognized my voice from the episode on the cell phone.

"It's our anniversary!" Roger's wife insisted. "Our thirty-first." *And this is all you got*, I thought. *Hell, at least I got red carpet and an X Caliber. All you get is a piece of fish.*

"Congratulations! You two look good together. What a wonderful couple. Any children?"

"Yes, four. Two girls and two boys."

"Wow, perfect match all the way around. Any grandchildren?"

"Just one."

"Beautiful, beautiful."

"You look familiar," I said to Roger, giving him a quick overview and then rolling my eyes. "Don't I know you?" I sat with my arms folded and waited for an answer.

"A lot of people say they know my husband," Roger's wife insisted, sounding proud of herself. "My husband is a popular man. He's the police captain in this district."

"Wonderful! I bet he's a good man. I'm sorry, but I didn't catch your name."

"Roberta. And you are?"

"Vera," I said, nice and slow. "Pleased to make your acquaintance. Now, back to you," I turned and said to the flushed red Roger, who seemed to be shitting bricks on himself. "I know exactly how I know you. You were at my house this morning."

"Wha–wha–wha?" he stuttered.

"Yeah, remember you came to let me know that you were now the head of the neighborhood crime watch?"

"Oh, yeah! Oh, yeah!"

Oh, I got your "oh, yeah" mu'fucker! Then I leaned to the side, threw my hip around in the tight-ass chair, and crossed my legs. To make the situation worse, I turned back toward my table, called Shannon, and invited her to come and bask in the glow.

"What's up, girl?" Shannon said as she kissed me on the cheek. Shannon only lived around the corner, so she arrived in less than five minutes.

"Is that who I think it is?" Shannon asked, tight-lipped. "Sho'ly is."

"What the hell is going on here?" Shannon asked, seeming amused.

"Roberta," I said, "this is my friend. I was just telling her that you've been married to—what's his name again? Oh, yeah, Roger—for thirty-one years today."

"Congratulations!" Shannon said enthusiastically. "Wonderful. It's not often you see a nice couple married for so long. So, tell me," Shannon asked, winking her eye at Roger. "What's your secret?"

"Love, honesty, and commitment," Roberta bragged, lying her ass off. "And friendship. There is nothing I don't know about my husband, and vice versa."

Yeah, right. "That's wonderful," I said. "Are you ladies married?"

"No," Shannon responded. "I'm scared my husband would be a cheat."

"Don't worry about those things. As long as you keep your man happy at home, he will have no reason to stray. And who knows? Maybe one day you young ladies will find someone just as special as my booga bear!"

Booga bear? Who is she fooling with her sad eyes and fake-ass smile? This huzzy must think I'm stupid. Please, I do believe I'll take my red velvet cake to go.

On the way out, I tapped Roberta on the shoulder and wished her good luck.

***

Ten minutes later, my cell phone rang. "Hello?"

"What the fuck do you think you're doing?" Roger said, blaring in my ear.

"Fuck you, Roger!"

"It wasn't what it looked like."

"Oh, no? Was I dreaming?"

"No. She heard me making reservations and she thought that I made them for her and me! What was I going to say? I had to take her. I had no choice."

"Look, this situation between us doesn't seem to be working out."

"Don't be like that, Vera!"

"What did I just say?"

"Let me make it up to you."

"How is that?"

"Manolo is having a sale."

"Shoes? You think you can make this up with shoes?"

"Okay, name it. What?"

"Nothing! We are done! Get it? Good-bye!"

I was pissed off, confused, and I felt guilty as hell. The truth is, I only snuck my ass to lunch because I was trying to run away from my feelings for Taj, and I only ended up running closer to him, because seeing Roger with his wife only made me want Taj even more.

I didn't know why I was running. I just I felt like I wanted to place my emotions on an airplane and run away with them. And where was I running to? I didn't know, especially when all of my needs, wants, and desires pointed toward Taj. I found myself looking for Taj in everything that I did. If I bought something to eat, I got enough for the both of us. If I bought something to wear, I wondered what he'd think. If I heard something funny, I savored the humor, as if I was holding my breath, and then I exhaled when I saw him, hopped in his lap, and told him what the joke was, and he just looked at me.

Something in his eyes smiled when I sat on his lap and lay in his arms. I felt safe, the same way I used to feel when Uncle Boy would hold my hand or take me to the park. At the same time, it was different because I outgrew Uncle Boy holding me, but I never wanted to let Taj go. I really couldn't deal with this.

Just then the phone rang. It was Roger.

"Vera," Roger said, "don't hang up, please. I'm really sorry about the other day. Please let me make it up to you."

"Spare me."

"Look, I fucked up, but come on, baby, just one more chance, please."

"Just this one time, Roger, but no more after this."

Two seconds after I said that, the doorbell rang. Roger was standing on my stoop, as if he had been sitting in front of my house waiting for me to invite him in.

Roger tried to kiss me when he walked in the door and handed me five hundred dollars. I nicely pushed him away and gave the money back to him.

"I'm cool," I said. "I don't want to be bothered with that anymore. Keep your money."

"Come on, baby," he said, running his hands across my breast.

"Would you get off of me?" I said, walking away and sitting on the couch.

"What's the problem, Vera?"

"There's no problem. I'm just not feeling you like that."

"What?"

"You heard me. You know what? Go home, Roger. Don't you have a wife and four kids? Go and see about them."

"You never worried about my wife and kids before."

"Well, things change and people change. I don't want to be with you anymore. I'm okay where I'm at." I stood up and he pushed me back down, trying to climb on top of me.

"So that's it?" he said. "We're done?"

"Roger, you are married. This shit couldn't go on forever! Now, get up!"

He pressed his chest deep into mine and pushed the hardness of his lower body into my abdomen and against my thighs.

"What the hell are you doing?" I said, trying to push him off of me.

"Fuck you!" Roger said, getting off of me. "I'm sick of you, you tramp-ass ho!"

"Whatever! Just get yo' shit and just leave!"

"Get my shit? You got a tow truck for the house, the car, and everything else around here that I bought?"

"If you don't stop talking stupid, I will hurt you. Now, get the fuck out and don't ever come back!"

"Oh, bitch, you gonna see me again!" Then he got up and left.

Immediately I jumped in the shower. I didn't want to smell like Roger when Taj came over.

I felt guilty when I saw Taj come through the door, and at that moment, I swore I would never see Roger again.

"What's wrong, Vera?" Taj asked as soon as he walked in the door and threw his stethoscope on the sofa. "What's the problem?"

"Who said I had a problem?"

"Your vibe. I saw the way you looked when I walked in here. Now, what's up?"

"I don't have a problem."

"Oh, here we go," he said, sitting down next to me. He placed my feet in his lap and started giving me a foot massage.

I snatched my feet away and placed them back on the floor. "Here we go?" I said. "Oh, so you really wanna know the problem?" I snapped. "This shit is the problem!"

"What shit?"

"This love situation between you and me."

"Oh, so that's it," he said, bending down and untying his sneakers.

"What's it?" I asked.

"Love?"

Love? Did he hear me say love? Did I say love? Well, maybe I did, but the more I was with Taj, the more I thought about Rowanda and starting over again, and having more emotion toward her than despise and disgust.

"I just can't take all of this closeness and you being in my personal space all the time!" I screamed out of frustration and anger. Goddamnit, what was going on? Loving this man was like an innate need to coexist with the silver lining of a dream, and the shit wasn't normal. What would happen when he left? He was going to leave, we all know that, but what would happen to me?

"Why do you keep pushing this love situation between us?" I said.

"There it goes again. You said love."

"All right, I said love! Dammit! Love."

"Oh, so you admit it?"

"Admit what?"

"That you love me?"

"Wait a minute. Let me clear this up. I never said that I loved you."

"Oh, so you don't love me?" he said with a look that said he felt anything but the opposite of his question.

"I don't even know how to be in love. Please, I have told so many niggas that I love them, just to get some shoes, a bag, a house, a car, a bank account. Hell, even a college and cosmetology degree. I have said I love you so much that I don't even know what it means. Hell, what is love anyway? Just a name?"

"Okay, now whatever that was you just said is done and over with. Get to the real shit, because I'm listening. And another thing, I'm getting a little tired of the tough girl routine. So you," he said, pointing, "better catch yourself! And another thing," he said before I could respond. "Did you go to lunch with Roger the other day?"

"No." I said, praying that he couldn't tell I was lying.

"Are you telling me the truth, Vera?"

"What did I just say? Why would I lie? Stop sweatin' me about that shit!"

"Sweatin' you? Why are you so defensive? Let me find out that you met Roger for lunch and see what happens."

"And what's going to happen?"

"I'ma leave your fuckin' ass, plain and simple."

I was two seconds away from slapping the shit out of him. "Who are you talking to?"

He looked around the room, with his arrogant ass, and said, "Do you happen to see someone else in here?"

"Oh, so, you're being smart?"

"Sometimes it's hard to tell whether I'm being smart or being stupid! The way you act at times, you'll make somebody hurt you."

"Ooooh, so now," I said, twisting my face, "you wanna hurt me? How could you love someone you wanna hurt?"

"Your mouth is what will make someone want to hurt you. But since you seem to be in dire need to change the subject, and you want to know why I love you, I'll tell you. I love you because every time I think, every time I breathe, I want it to be with you. I love being around you, the joy that you bring, the excitement of your spirit. I love you because the love you have for me is straight the hell up, and you're not trying to be with me just because you hit a gold mine, because if the truth be told, you haven't asked me for jack!"

"So, what does that mean? And another thing, your li'l punk ass reason for love is weak! Because if I loved you, it would be because I've never met anyone like you, I've never felt the challenge of the heart, and being with you makes me think about brand new beginnings. And yes, I gotta thing for you! And yes, I no longer just like you, I'm straight feeling you, but so the fuck what? I'm still not committing to you."

"You know what, baby? I just figured it out," he said. "I need to give you exactly what you've been asking for, time and space. I'm not the one, sweetheart. I have less problems in the hospital emergency room than I have with you. When you grow up, call me. Until then, remember your little don't-hate-the-player-hate-the-game line, and be sure to apply it to yourself!" He picked up his running Nikes, slipped them on his feet, threw on his throwback jersey, and headed for the door.

"Where are you going?"

"I'm going to give you some time. You're not ready."

"Ready for what?"

"For me."

"You haven't even given me a chance," I heard myself saying, which was the complete opposite of what I meant to say, which was "Kiss my ass."

"I give you a chance every day, Vera. Give me a minute to think. This shit is too much!"

He slammed the door when he left, and my three-hundred-dollar silk pillows ended up getting tear stains after all.

But this time, I couldn't let him go. I ran through the living room and snatched the front door open. He was standing on the front stoop.

"Look Taj," I said, breathing heavy and out of breath. "I'll try, okay? I'll try."

Step Six

The gossip hour/book club meeting with the girls was exactly what I needed. I hadn't spent any quality time with them since Lee blew up Pastor James's spot. Shannon insisted that we have the meeting at her house, although we had no book to discuss.

"You were layin' it down, girlfriend. Seems like Roger couldn't deal," Shannon insisted, while sucking the ice cream off her spoon.

"Seems like it," Angie insisted. "His ass was pussy whipped!"

"You three are about as educated as tramps can be," Lee said, adding her two cents in."You shouldn't be messing with nobody's husband anyway!"

"Lets not forget," I reminded Miz Thing, "people in glass houses, et cetera, et cetera."

"Nowadays," Shannon said, cutting me off, "it's hard to find a man that will give up the dick with no strings attached."

"No you didn't," I insisted. "How long have I been telling you that? Men are not like they used to be."

"I know," Shannon agreed. "Now, they're the ones that want a commitment and want to be in relationships."

"You see where I'm going with this, right?"

"I feel you, girlfriend," Angie said. "My ex-husband still trying to get back with me."

"Oh, no he's not!" I said.

"Yes, he is, but I told him hell no. Stay in L.A. and take care of Bey-Bey and the rest of the get-along gang. Just send me my alimony check!"

"A high five to that! I'm wit' you, girlfriend." Shannon laughed.

"Well, girls," Shannon continued, "I have to admit something to you."

"Bitch, you better not be pregnant. You know that pregnant shit is contagious!" Angie screamed.

"Don't be stupid! Quincy is going to be moving in with me."

Did this heifer just say Quincy? Shannon and Quincy were Aunt Cookie and Uncle Boy in the making. Every other goddamn week they were in love, and in between those times, she couldn't stand his ass. Too much drama, if you ask me. I told her a long time ago to fuck him and keep it movin', but nevertheless, here we went again.

"What the hell is wrong with you?" I had to know.

"Nothing is wrong with me, I just figured that Quincy is good for me."

"Weren't you just talking about how you can't find dick with no strings attached?" I snapped. "What did he do so great this week that makes you wanna live with him?"

"First of all, Miss Dick Hound, I owe you no explanation as to why I want my man living with me. Nobody has said anything to you about your undercover brother and your in-house dick! You ain't slick, and I don't know about you, but I'm thirty-one and will soon be thirty-two. Folks can hear my biological clock ticking all the way in Afghanistan. And yes, I still believe that you can't find decent dick with no strings attached, but that ain't got shit to do with Quincy."

"Are you crazy, Shannon?" Angie snapped. "I've been married, and believe me, there's no way you wanna look at the same goddamn man every day," she slurred, as if saying the words made her tired. "Trust me. Men get comfortable. Either they think you're their mama or they feel their yo' daddy. Men take breastfeeding to a whole 'nother level!"

"Well," Lee interjected, "I don't see anything wrong with commitment. All men are not alike."

"You're sure right," I said. "Some are nice, but dumb as hell, and some are smart, but just irk the shit outta you!"

"Amen," Angie said. "And some are sweet in bed, but jacked up in the head, and some have it straight in the head, but jacked up in the bed."

"See, Angie," I said, "you get my point."

"Mm-hmm, and when you are dealing with the fine descendants of the Zulu, Ashanti, Ibo, Yoruba, tight packer, loose packer, and Chicken George tribes, it requires lots of emotionally filled time."

"Time I don't have," Angie said.

"Well, I do," Shannon said, "and I think that living with Quincy is the best decision that I can make for my future."

"Well, do you, boo, 'cause I'm sick of the mu'fuckers myself. I can't find a decent man to save my goddamn life."

"Shannon," Lee said, "I thought you said Angie had a profile online."

"Oh, no you didn't, bitch!" Angie screamed. "I told you not to say anything!"

"I only told Lee," Shannon said, "and Vera, but that was it. I didn't tell anybody else. So, you may as well tell them what went down. I was too embarrassed to let the shit out myself."

"All right," Angie said, rolling her eyes. "Y'all know I ain't had no dick in months, since the episode with the li'l twenty-year-old at the ice cream parlor. So, needless to say, I been lonely as hell, and I figured, fuck it. It's 2004, the new millennium. I'll try and date online. Plus I figured I was equipped, being that I have a few degrees in men."

"What degree? O.P.P.?" I said, laughing.

"Fuck you Vera. I don't do that shit anymore."

"Well, what other degrees in men do you have?" I asked.

"I have *Dog*-ology," she responded. "*Cheatin'*-ology, and *Busted*-ology also. Then there's the *I'm-sorry*-ology, and the *No, I don't want to get back together*-ology, and some of these I have earned two or three times."

"Damn, and I thought I was bad," I said, shaking my head.

"Anyway," she continued, "I chatted online with all kinds of men, but there was this one that captured my attention. He lived here in Brooklyn and was self-employed. My only worry with meeting him online was that he might've been fat. Lord knows I can't deal with no fat man, especially since I've got my own set of chubby-like problems."

"Would you tell the story?" Shannon said.

"All right, well, after a few chats and one tele-
phone conversation, I thought Daddy-O.com
seemed pretty trustworthy, so we set a date and
agreed to meet at Soul Café. I was so excited to be
going out that I wore my best one-piece strapless
bra and girdle combo, my apple green chiffon
halter top dress, and my Cinderella high heel
mules. Daddy-O.com and I—Eugene was actually
his name—decided to meet in the parking lot
before going in to have dinner.

"At first, I saw a couple of guys who I thought
may have been Eugene, however, as I got closer,
they either walked away or stood back and looked
at my ass. I knew that Eugene and I agreed on
seven-thirty, and he assured me that he was a
stickler for promptness. But it was five minutes
after eight and no Eugene. He said that he drove
a dark green Windstar, but the only Windstar
that I saw was parked in a handicap parking
space. After about five minutes of standing
around and looking for Eugene, I heard someone calling my name: *Angela, Angela Adams.
It's me, Eugene.*

"Well, divas, when I turned around and looked,
Eugene was about three and a half feet from the
ground! My Lord! Truthfully, his height didn't
bother me as much as the patch over his right
eye, which he felt a need to lift up to show me

how the eye underneath wandered and caused him to see me going round and round. Which, by the way, he thought was funny.

"During dinner, Eugene seemed to be quite intelligent, and If I could have gotten over the fact that he required a booster seat and the patch over his eye, he wouldn't have been half bad. Once dinner was over and the bill came, Eugene explained that his patch caused him to see only half of the menu's prices, and that he wasn't going to pay sixty dollars for anybody to eat! And to add insult to injury, he told me that had he known I would be so expensive and not have any consideration for the afflicted, that he would have left my lonely ass home.

"Bastard! I left his half-seeing ass there! I started to yank his booster seat from under him, but instead, I jumped in my car and headed home. And since that time, with the exception of the li'l boy at the ice cream parlor and the li'l security guard, I've been sitting on my custom designed leather sofa, in the comfort of my Afrocentric living room, adding to my collection of Annie Lee figurines and waiting for Santa Claus to drop Prince Charming off at my house."

"Damn girl," Lee said, trying to stop herself from laughing. "Tell us about the eye going round and round again."

I cracked up! As I wiped the tears out of my eyes from laughing so hard, my cell phone rang. Shannon, Angie, and Lee stopped their conversation and were dead in my mouth.

"Hi Taj," I said, answering the phone.

"Can you skate, Vera?"

I couldn't believe he asked me if I could skate. Hell, all ghetto kids can skate. Even if you only had one skate and learned to skate by holding onto the back of a bike, skating was as innate as survival, and here I had Mr. Fine-ass Yuppie calling me and asking me if I can skate!

"The question is, can you skate?" I asked him.

"Oh, you're challenging my skills?"

"Yo' skills? What skills? The ones from the hospital?"

"Hold up. You think I was born and raised in the hospital. My first word wasn't *doctor*."

"Yeah, right. What was it, *nurse*?" I said, and then mouthing to Angie, Lee, and Shannon to get out of my mouth!

"Understand this, I might not look like the hood," Taj said, "but I'm certainly from the hood. And though you may think differently, you weren't the only one eating choke sandwiches and government cheese. So, please, just name a time and place, throw your skates on, and let's get it goin'!"

"The hood, please," I said. "I'm not talking about a bad street in a nice neighborhood. I'm talking about niggas just runnin' the place. About the bar on the corner, the hustler on the move, and the old lady down the street whippin' ass! I'm talking about ghettofied love, baby. That's the hood."

"Sweetheart," he said, trying to talk over the back and forth paging of the hospital intercom, "you ain't said nothin' but a word. Brick City, baby! Represent! Brick City!"

Now, I just about died laughing when he said that. "You better quiet that down before the rest of the doctors start hiding their shit, thinking they about to get jacked up in there! You need your job, baby. Don't scare the white people."

"All right. All right. I lost a little control for a moment," he said, sounding as if he was straightening up his pointed polo collar, and now sounding more astute than the episode he just had. "You know what they say, you can take the man out the ghetto, but you can't take the ghetto out the man."

"Or the doctor, in your case. Meet me at seven at the skating rink uptown."

I must have had the word *cheese* written across my face for the remainder of the meeting, because Shannon kept telling me to close my mouth. Taj had just cracked me the hell up. Imagine a thugged-out yuppie skating. That shit is classic!

After I left Shannon's, I hurried home to shower and change, then I left back out so that I could meet Taj. I had on my tight leather shorts and the matching top. I had my Christian Dior sports bag, and I was sharp as shit when I arrived at the skating rink.

When I pulled up, Taj was standing outside waiting for me. He walked over, kissed me on the lips, and said, "Damn, girl, why in the hell you wanna do this to a brotha?"

"What?"

He took my hand and placed it on his dick. It was so hard that I could almost feel the veins bulging out.

I started to smile, and I looked at him and said, "It's all good. It lets me know that a sista is handling her business."

"But, damn, why do have to handle it right here?" He pulled me against his chest and said, "Let me get a quickie."

"You can't be serious."

"For real. R.Kelly wrote 'Sex in My Jeep' for a reason."

I mushed him playfully on the side of his head and said, "I'll lay it down for you later. Now stop being fresh. The kids standing across the street," I said, pointing, "are watching you feel all over my ass."

He stepped back, looked me up and down, and said, "The skating rink is that way."

I smiled, and the sweet scent of his body lingered in my nose. His gear was tight; I must admit. He had on a Knicks throwback jersey, baggy carpenter jeans, and blue Tims.

"I see you feeling to go back to your roots, Mr. Brick City," I said. "'Cause you thugged-out as hell!"

He smiled. "This little routine you have going on here is adorable, but put your skates on and let's see what you can do."

"Oh, you got jokes? Well, let me see if your feet work as well as your mouth does!"

The music in this place was slammin'! I hadn't heard "One Night Love Affair" and "Ten Percent" since I was twenty-three and hanging out in the Peppermint Lounge in Jersey. So, when "Follow Me" came on, I had to do my thing on the floor! And honey, while the disco ball was twirling around and all the people were gettin' down, you couldn't tell whether I was Stella, Vera, or a Don Cornelius disco diva. All right!

"Oh, I see you have some skills!" Taj said, standing back and admiring my groove. "Well,

Miz Thang, watch this," he said as the music changed from "Follow Me" to The Jungle Brothers' "Girl, I'll House You."

Don't you know that this so-'n-so did a split with them baggy-ass pants on, and then pulled himself up and took off with the roller-skating version of the moonwalk.

Oh, hell no. I know he doesn't think that he can outdo me!

Check this out, I broke out with a Michael Jackson kick and a nasty-girl snake. The next thing I heard, the DJ had changed from the Jungle Brothers to the Cha-Cha Slide, and everybody and their mama rushed to do the roller skating version of the Charlie Brown! All right now!

Then there was the kickoff of all roller skating get downs, the roller skating version of the stepper's dance! This was straight on and poppin'. So, when the young lady rolled up to me, tapped me on the shoulder, and said, "May I speak to you for a moment?" I ain't think shit of it.

Taj didn't even notice. He said he had to go to the bathroom, and for me to hold that step because he would be right back.

"May I help you?" I asked, breathing heavy, but smiling at the same time.

"Who are you?" she asked.

"Excuse me?" Now I was pretty much taken aback. I figured at most this heifer was admiring my gear and wanted to know where I got the Donna Karan leather shorts from.

"Look, I'ma get right to the point," she said with a straight face to let me know there was no bullshit between us. "That guy you were just dancing with is my man."

"What? Taj?"

"Yes, Taj. I understand that he's cool and all, and him being a doctor will attract a lot of groupies, but from one sista to the next, respect my place and step off!" Then she topped it off with a Barbie-doll smile.

Well, you know ole girl, so as you can imagine, I was 'bout to read her, and right at the point where I went to tell the bitch about how, if he was her man, he sure could eat a good pussy, I changed my mind.

"You know what, sista? I'ma let you get that for the moment, because I respect your forward-ness. But check this, when Taj comes back, we will speak to him together." Then I hit her ass right back with her fake-ass Barbie smile. "By the way, what's your name?"

"Ja . . . mil . . . lah," she said, nice and slow with an exuberant amount of confidence.

Taj came back, and he still didn't notice Jamillah standing next to me. He took me by both my arms and pulled me close. "You look good as hell, girl," he said playfully. "What's your name, and do you have a man?"

"My name," I said, backing away from his embrace, "is Vera, but her name is Ja . . . mil . . . lah. And do I have a man? Well, the one I thought I had, she said is hers."

He was shocked as hell, but then the doctor, non-chalant, non-emotional shit kicked in and he said, "How are you, Jamillah?"

"How am I? How am I?" she asked with a chuckle of disbelief. "I was quite well until I got here," she responded.

"Really? Would you like to talk about it?"

"What the fuck is going on here?" Jamillah said with her neck in full motion. "Taj, why are you playing games? You think this shit is funny?"

"What's funny?"

"Taj, it was my understanding that you were my man, so what are you doing out with someone else? Don't you feel the slightest bit busted?"

"I feel a little odd and awkward, because I would have never set up a meeting like this, but for you to say that I'm your man is way off course."

"Off course!" the bitch shouted.

Now, usually I woulda jumped in, but not this time. This nigga had to wear this one, 'cause had I gotten into it, I woulda punched the bitch in her face first and talked later.

"Whose house were you at the other night?" Jamillah asked.

"Yours."

My heart cracked when he said that, but I played it cool and stood there.

"Well, then," she said, more to me than to him.

"But what does that mean?" Taj asked

"Excuse you?"

"Listen, let's get this straight now. There's no you and I. There was no you and I the other night, tonight, or tomorrow, for that matter. You and I haven't slept together. You're good people, a nice conversation, but that's it. I'm embarrassed that you're even acting like this. So, check it. You're not my lady, my girlfriend, or anything else that involves commitment, so stop telling people that!"

Well, that did it for me! Now I was pissed the fuck off! "People? People? Oh, hell no, mu'fucker. My name is Vera," I said, looking dead in ole boy's grill. "Furthermore," I said, feeling like I was going to break, "she doesn't owe me any explanations."

"Look, boo," I turned to her and said. "If this is your man, then place a red bow on top of his head, because you can have him! I'm outta here!"

"Get your ass back here!" Taj demanded, with his left jaw thumpin'. He then grabbed me tight by my forearm. "Stand still! I'm tired of you running. You're not going anywhere! You will listen to what I have to say, and when you leave out that door, it'll be the same way you came in here. With me!"

I do believe that if Jamillah could've caught me sleeping and gut-punched my ass, the ho would've tried it. She stood there speechless, while Taj totally ignored her, trying to get me to stand next to him.

"So, that's how it is, Taj?" Jamillah said, breaking her silence.

"That's how it's been!"

"Fuck you!" she screamed, roller skating off.

"And fuck you too, bitch!"

"And you," Taj said, turning toward me, "don't you ever let anyone come up in yo' face and question your position with me! You supposed to be so tough, but you let this chick punk you into backing me into a corner, then you try and leave me standing here with her. What kind of weak-ass game is that? I thought you had yo' shit covered!

"You got issues, you know that? You made these rules, and now you can't live by them. Let me tell you something. You see this game shit you got going on over here, I got it down pat, and I told you once before, you cannot out hustle me, so stop trying! And when you lay down laws and you say shit like 'don't hate the player, hate the game,' you have to be able to work that shit! Don't be scared! What, you can't hang? Isn't this what you wanted? The flip side of the game?"

After we left the roller skating rink, Taj and I were silent for most of the night, other than to make love, which I guess was a conversation in and of itself. I mean, really, what was I going to say? Why did I let myself fall in love with you? This shit was suddenly beyond my control, and for the first time in a long time, Vera Wright-Turner was speechless. All I could do was watch this man and try not to think about Rowanda, about Grandma, or about Lincoln Street. All I wanted on my mind was me and my man. And for the moment, where you can take your index finger and go pop, was about the length of time I was able to make this accomplishment.

For most of my life, Aunt Cookie would never let me forget who my mother was, which was why she didn't allow me to call her Mommy. Even when she would refer to me as her daughter, and she knew that I loved her like a mother, she would always say, "I don't want you to forget Rowanda. You're with me because she loved you."

Then she would say, "Your mother is as much a part of you as you are a part of you."

I would always cry and feel like I was never good enough for anybody to be my mother, and then, much like I am now, I would think about Lincoln Street and about the time when Grandma's man held me down, the same man that was there when she died.

He came in the bedroom, walked over to me, twirled my braids, and told me how pretty I looked with my "fat ass" and "chubby li'l pussy." Nobody said a word.

"You gonna have to wear this one," he said. "Nobody told you to be coming in here looking at me like that."

"But I ain't seen you today. I been in here looking out the window."

"You been in the other room looking at me," he said. "Lay down or I'll kill ya."

Shortly after that, Rowanda tried to kill Grandma's man. When Rowanda came home from jail, I saw her sitting on the bench in the middle of the courtyard.

"Where you been, Rowanda?" I yelled, while doing a summersault across the bench that sat in front of Building 251A.

"I been gone," she said.

"Gone where?"

"To jail, baby."

"I ain't no baby."

"You my baby," she insisted.

"Yo' baby? I ain't got no mama. You ain't my mama. You'se a crackhead."

Before I could shake my thoughts about being raped and come back to the present, Taj rolled on top of me and started running his hands between my thighs and sucking on my breast. I tensed up. He had started kissing down the middle of my stomach and making his way to my thighs when he realized that my body was stiff.

He lifted his head up, rolled over, and said, "Tell me what's wrong."

"Nothing," I said with a slight tremble. "Why did you stop?"

"Because you wanted me to."

"I never said that," I said, looking away from him.

"Look at me," he said. "I'm talking to you. Now, tell me the truth."

"Nothing is wrong, Taj!" I snapped.

"Vera, usually when I suck on your breast, kiss you on your stomach, and get ready to go down and taste you, your body melts. I know your body better than I know my own. Now, tell me what you were thinking, and don't lie. You were thinking about when you were a little girl weren't you?"

"Yes," I said, looking away.

"Look at me. I'm right here."

I looked at him, and tears started to build in my eyes. "When I was a little girl," I said, "my grandmother's man raped me, the same one that was there when she died. The same man that splashed in the puddle of her blood and left his footprint. I bled for days after he raped me, and when Rowanda came home, she noticed that I had blood running down my legs. She took me to the hospital, and they told her that I had been raped."

Taj started biting his bottom lip, and his eyes became glassy. "What did Rowanda do?" he asked.

"She carried me home from the hospital, placed me in the bed, and went in the kitchen with Grandma and her man. She grabbed a knife and stabbed him twenty times. The only thing that stopped her was when Grandma beat her in the head. After that, Grandma called the police, and Rowanda was arrested. She spent eighteen months in prison." My shoulders started to shake. I couldn't hold the tears in any longer. I started to cry.

"It's over, baby," Taj said, kissing my tears. "You're mine now."

Taj held me in between his arms, and I felt safe lying against his chest. "Vera, I swear to God," he said, "if I could find that motherfucka, I would kill him!"

"Shh," I said. "Don't say that." I could feel Taj tighten his embrace as I lay my head on his chest and I fell asleep.

When the phone rang, I jumped. I looked up at Taj, and I could see he had been watching me while I was asleep. He kissed me on my forehead and pressed the speaker button on the phone. "Hello," he said.

"Come on over here and let Aunt Cookie grease your scalp," Aunt Cookie said, not realizing at first that Taj was the one who answered the phone. "Wait a minute. Hello?"

"How are you?" Taj said.

"Who is this?"

"Taj."

"Hey, Babyboy, show me whatcha workin' wit'! Where is my Vera?"

"Right here."

"Oh, 'cause I'll fuck 'em up!" She laughed. "You know how I do it!"

Taj took the phone off the receiver and handed me the earpiece while he clicked off the speaker option.

"I see Taj sticking around." Aunt Cookie chuckled. "Don't go jumping the gun."

"He answering your phone and you telling me not to jump the gun? Hell, the way I see it, the only thing left is to jump the broom."

"Anyway, Aunt Cookie, as soon as I get dressed I'll be over there."

When I got up to get dressed, Taj lay in the bed and watched me stroll around the room naked.

"What are you looking at?" I said, teasing him.

"You."

"Why?"

"'Cause right now, I feel like I want to protect you from the world."

"Taj, don't worry about me. Believe me when I tell you I can take care of myself. Now, go to sleep. You know you have a long shift coming up."

By the time I got ready to leave, Taj had fallen asleep. I kissed him on the forehead before I left.

***

Aunt Cookie was sitting on her front stoop when I got there. She already had the grease and the comb on the ledge, waiting for me like she used to when I was a little girl and she would braid my hair. We used to sit on the porch, while Uncle Boy sat on the bottom step shootin' craps with his friends, playing cards, or simply drinking an ice cold beer. I used to love those times.

I smiled when I saw Aunt Cookie, and I walked up the stairs to where she was and gave her a hug and told her that I loved her.

I nestled my head in the creases of Aunt Cookie's soft thigh, while holding the jar of black Dax grease. She reached for a finger full to place on the back of her hand.

"You think Rowanda ever been clean?" I asked her.

"Depends on what you mean by clean. You mean, ever had a clean path or ever had a clean mind, a clean dream, or ever been clean from a crack pipe or a dope needle?"

"Clean of everything."

"Nobody is clean of everything, at least not in these parts. I always say, 'There but for the grace of God, go I.' Aunt Cookie have done a lot of things in her day. Some things folks know about, and some things folks don't, but it all made me who I am today.

"Rowanda never been shown how to be clean. She never knew not to be turned out, never knew not to jones for love, or not to jones for drugs."

"What does that mean?"

"Rowanda never been clean. Your grandmother carried on generations of hurt and pain, caused by somebody daddy or mama who died long ago.

"Rowanda used to beg for money on the street, and Larry used to feed her. He would give her money 'cause he was a big time drug dealer. Larry ain't never gave a shit 'bout nobody but Larry, and somehow Rowanda got mixed up in there. Larry put her on the block, made her hustle her ass, and instead of cash, he offered her stash—a stash of dreams that would take her away from her day-to-day existence."

In the midst of being told all of this, for a brief moment, I wasn't disgusted when I saw Rowanda walking up Aunt Cookie's stoop with a red bandana on, an oversized and out of shape green T-shirt, and too big jeans. I looked at her and thought that I could love her for a moment, despite the track marks and the Budweiser beer can in her hand.

"Hey, Cook!" she said.

"Hello, Vee."

"Vera," I said sternly, to correct her.

Aunt Cookie slightly nudged me on the side of my head, as she yanked a part of my hair with the comb. "Hey, Rowanda. How you been? You looking good, girl," Aunt Cookie said, lying.

"I been to this methadone clinic, and they said that they gonna set me up with this program when they have a bed."

"A bed? Methadone? I thought you were a crackhead," I said, feeling the same way I felt when I was seven and flipping summersaults across the park bench, feeling like she wasn't shit.

"I might be, but I'm still your mother."

"You ain't my mu'fuckin' mother!" I screamed.

"Then who is your mother?"

"I ain't got no goddamn mother!"

"You got a mother, and she a fiend who ain't shit."

"I will break yo' mu'fuckin' ass!" Aunt Cookie said to me, pointing the comb in my face and delivering words like stab wounds. "Don't you ever stand up here and disrespect your mother like this! Now apologize!"

"I wish I would!" Before I could stomp off the stoop, Aunt Cookie had slapped me, but I didn't cry. Instead, I gathered my things and I left.

Step Seven

"Hey, Vee," Rowanda said, coming into the shop, slightly well dressed, with gray jeans and a white blouse on. Her hair was braided, going straight to the back with zigzag parts in between them. She looked as if she had taken the time she needed to wash her face and clear her mind. For the first time since she came in Grandma's house and had three bags of legitimate groceries, she walked with a strut. Somebody told Aunt Cookie that she managed to maintain a thirty-day detox program and was somehow into God.

She didn't bother to heed the fact that the sign on the door said closed when she waltzed herself in and called me Vee, knowing good and well that was my project name, and I didn't want to hear it anymore. She was pretty for once, and for the first time in my life, I could accept that she and I looked alike. Her voice was sultry soft and reminded me of how she and Phyllis Hyman shared the same gift of lyrical speech.

"Hey, Vee," she said. "I wanted to come and let you know I was clean."

"Clean of what?"

"Of shit. Of garbage. Of all them drugs that's been runnin' my life. I'm clean." She said this frantically, as if she had just taken a hot shower or a warm bath, as if she needed me to see that she somehow had a cleanliness that I could feel.

"That's nice," I said nonchalantly, "but what are you telling me for?"

"Vee, I've changed. I changed for you. I know that you only wanted me to be clean. Well, I'm here."

For a moment, I talked myself outta breaking down and crying. Instead, I bit my lip and repeated my question. "Why are you telling me?"

"'Cause I want you to know."

"Well, now I know, so you can leave."

She stood there and stared.

I felt like a volcano was preparing to explode. I grabbed my black leather midriff jacket, my Kate Spade leopard print bag, and walked the hell out. I stood on the other side of the glass picture window and motioned for her to come out of my shop or I would call the police.

She didn't even seem to care. She held her head up high and said, "I'm still your mother." That was her good-bye. The same good-bye she gave me when the pink Aries K, filled with social workers, came and dragged me down the street.

I started to think about the day that social services came and took me away when Grandma died. My cousins, Dirty and Biggie, had run away. They were supposed to take me with them, but they changed their minds and left without me.

The mattress in Rowanda's room was on the floor. It was old and gray with faded blue stripes. There were no sheets to cover it, but she had towels on it so that I wouldn't have to lay on the bare mattress. I lay balled up in a fetal position, and Rowanda snatched me out of the bed.

"Here she go," Rowanda said to the well-dressed lady standing behind her. "Y'all ain't got to make no big scene. I know I ain't fit to keep her."

"What is you doin', Rowanda?" I said, stumbling to the floor half asleep.

"See this lady," Rowanda said. "This is a social worker. She came to take you. You gotta go."

I was silent as I looked around the room. I couldn't believe that Rowanda was giving me away after all I did to love her. After all I tried to do. I never told anybody that she smoked the pipe at night or snuck out to be with a man. I never told anybody that she left me alone all night long, so for the life of me, I couldn't figure out why she wouldn't want me anymore.

The social worker stood behind Rowanda, and she held her hand out for me to grab a hold of it. When she saw that I wasn't coming toward her, she started walking toward me and calling my name. I ran and grabbed Rowanda around the knees and begged her to please keep me.

"I'ma be good, Rowanda. I promise. I won't fight no more, and I'll try real hard not to cuss."

"Be quiet, Vera," Rowanda said. "You ain't that bad. Matter of fact, you ain't done nothin'. Now, get up! This has to do with me and not you."

"Rowanda, look," I said, letting go of her knees and running past the social worker to the empty rusted coffee can that I kept pennies in. "Here, take these!" I was moving so fast that I tripped over my own feet and the pennies splattered all over the wooden floor. I scurried around to pick them up, handing them to Rowanda one by one. Tears fell from my eyes as I ran around the room.

"Here, Rowanda," I said. "Take this money and buy us some food. Take it all, please! I won't tell nobody that you smoked up all your money. I won't say nothing. I know I be too fresh. I know I'm bad, but I'm sorry. You forgive me?

All theses pennies together make at least three dollars. That's enough for some bologna and cheese, maybe even some bread. Now, please, can I stay?"

Rowanda bent down on her knees, started crying, and said, "Vera, I'ma always be your mother, but you have to go with this lady."

"But I don't wanna go!" I cried. "I just gave you the money. You always say we don't have no money, so I been finding pennies and saving them. That's all the money I got. What else you need? Please don't let them take me." I started hugging her around her neck and squeezing tight.

The social worker placed her hand on my arm and I bit it! "Get offa me!" I yelled, "I wanna stay with my mother!"

Rowanda pushed me off and said, "Vera, look at me. I'm a fiend. They ain't gonna let me keep you!"

"But I don't wanna go, Rowanda. Mommy, please," I begged. "Mommy, I'll be good. Mommy, don't make me go."

"You ain't done nothin'! And I already told you not to call me Mommy. I can't take being called that knowing that I can't take care of you. Now, stop it! You ain't done nothin' but be born. I'm the one that's the dog in this life, and they is not gonna let me keep you!"

"But why not?"

"I just told you that I'm a fiend, girl!"

"So, ain't everybody 'cept the school teacher and the social worker a fiend?"

"No, girl, everybody is not no fiend. Now, let's go!"

I kicked and screamed, while Rowanda carried me down the stairs with my legs wrapped around her waist and my arms squeezing her neck tight. "Rowanda, please! I'll find some more money. I promise. Now, let me stay! Pretty please."

Rowanda peeled me off of her and handed me to the social worker. The police were standing there, and they warned Rowanda that if she tried anything, they would arrest her. Rowanda stood there an gave a snort. She watched me bang on the windows and thrash around the back seat of the car as I tried to get out. She watched, and then she turned to walk away.

"I'm still yo' mother," she said to me as she started walking down the street. "I'm still your mother, and don't you ever forget that."

By now, my memories had my chest feeling like it was going to cave in. I wiped the tears that were flowing from my eyes like rain, and I swallowed the hard lump in my throat. I banged on the dashboard and forced myself to remember that I was no longer the same eight-year-old girl, swinging my body around in the back seat.

I jumped out of my truck and yelled down the street after Rowanda, "You ain't my fuckin' mother!" It was something that I couldn't do when I was eight, but now that I was thirty-one, I could make up for lost time, so I continued to scream, "You ain't my fuckin' mother!" Then I revved up my truck up and took off as fast as I could.

While waiting at the traffic light, my cell phone rang. "Vera!" Shannon was screaming, while I was struggling to place the earpiece in my cell phone. Shannon was breathing heavy and crying, which instantly made me nervous.

"Quincy!" she said. "Quincy was waiting outside of my office and he saw me kiss Nile!"

"What? Nile? Quincy saw you kiss Nile? Big deal. You better not own up to that shit. If Quincy didn't tap you on the shoulder and say, 'Hey, Shannon, it's me,' then don't you confess to nothing."

"But he told me he was going to kill me when I got home!"

"What?"

"That's what he said, all because of Nile! Vera, you don't understand. I love this man."

"Who? Nile?"

"No, dammit! I love Quincy!" she yelled. "Will you listen to me?"

"I'm trying to, but you're confusing me. And who the hell is Nile?"

"He's a friend of mine."

"When you get a new friend?"

"Like a couple of weeks ago."

"Quincy just moved in with you a couple of weeks ago."

"I know, but still."

"But still what? You meeting friends that you can kiss?"

"Nile was a very close friend."

"Mm-hmm. Don't give me the shit. Hit me with the real deal, Shannon."

"Look, the mu'fucker was fine," she admitted. "He had big hands, big feet, and he was black as hell. I wanted to do 'im. I can't even lie. Every time I saw him, I wanted to fuck him. He has an office in the same building as my magazine. We used to ride the elevator together."

"Did you fuck him in the elevator?"

"No, but I wanted to. I love Quincy, but now I'm scared. I can't go home! Quincy is crazy. You know he used to sell drugs, right? Plus, his hand's like the size of my face. Please, Vera, I need you. I can't go to a gunfight with a knife!"

"You can't cheat worth a damn. What kinda high school game yo' ass playing? You don't never have the maintenance man anywhere near your job, knowing you got a crazy nigga at home. I'm sorry, Shannon, but Quincy's ass is too big for me to fuck up. You got a mu'fuckin' problem on yo' hands."

"I'll admit I fucked up, all right, but I need help, Vera!"

I could have strangled Shannon. "Meet me on Lincoln Street," I said.

When I met up with Shannon, I saw Rowanda walking down the street, but I looked the other way. Then I saw my cousins, Dirty and Biggie, hustling the block from the front seat of their kitted-up ride, with the convertible roof down and Snoop Dog pumpin' inside. The way they sat with long braids in their hair, clean white wife beaters on, and brown corduroy shoes, you would have thought that they were from Long Beach or Compton.

"What up, cuz?" Dirty asked, boppin' his head and signing Warren G's hook on "Gin and Juice."

"What up, cuz?" he asked. "Remember this? This shit is knockin'!"

"My girl and I got a li'l situation here," I said.

"What? Some niggas? Some bitches? Not to worry. Yo' cousins got the shit locked!" Dirty insisted. "You better take that down, Chief," Biggie said.

"Mu'fucka, please!" Quincy replied. "Step off! As a matter of fact, y'all need to disappear before I lose my mind and shoot a nigga!"

"Fuck that," Dirty said. "My cousin called me over here 'cause they had a problem with yo' ass. Now, you need to be gettin' yo' shit so you can jet."

Quincy stopped packing his things and looked at Shannon. "Whose fuckin' idea was it to bring Frick and Frack and put them in my face?"

"Vera's," she said, nudging me on the arm.

Oh, no this bitch didn't just say that. I musta heard wrong.

"What did you just say, Shannon?" I said.

"Well, it was your idea. I don't know them."

Well, I'll be damned! "You know what? Fuck it. Dirty, Biggie," I turned to them and said, "I'm sorry, go home. This chick doesn't know whether she's coming or going."

"You sure, cuz?" Dirty asked.

"Yeah, I'm sure."

They got back in their car and took off.

"Look, Quincy," Shannon said, "I'm in love with you, and I don't want you to go. It wasn't what you thought."

"Then what was it, Shannon?" he asked.

"I was just giving him a hug. He's one of Vera's old boyfriends. Right, Vera?"

Oh, now the bitch expects me to lie after she turned on me. "Mm-hmm, whatever," I said, pissed off.

Shannon shot me the evil eye. "Let's just try." She turned to Quincy and said, "We owe each other that much."

"I need a minute to breathe, Shannon. I really do." Then he got in his truck and took off.

Step Eight

"Well, the next time you'll mind your business," Taj said.

"You had no reason to be up in Quincy's face anyway. That's Shannon's man."

"Shannon is my best friend."

"Yeah, but Quincy is not your man. Your man is right here, and your man is telling you to stay out of that the next time. You see how the shit ended up."

Before I could respond, the phone rang. "He's back!" Shannon was blaring in my ear as soon as I picked up the phone, not even waiting for me to say hello. "What should I do?"

Taj pointed toward the door to let me know he was going to the bathroom. "Who's back?" I asked Shannon.

"Quincy!" she shouted.

"Is he pissed off?"

"A little, but he's not angry. He's a workable pissed off."

"Okay, what now?" I asked.

"I want him back," she said.

"Okay, well, act sick."

"What?"

"Yeah, act sick. Cough real loud, act like you have to hog spit phlegm all the time, like this, awwh, hack! Awwh, hack!"

"I'm not hog spittin' no damn phlegm. Are you crazy? I wanna screw his ass when this is all over with, not have him looking at me like I got STD of the mouth! Plus, I want this man. I'ma sit his ass down and tell him the truth. Lay it all on the line before I'm left alone for good."

"There you go, being stupid. You have to think like a man. A cheatin' man don't tell yo' ass shit that you don't already know. Even when you catch him in the act, by the time he's done telling the story, it's something different. Don't you go admitting to anything. Just listen to what he has to say, and if he doesn't bring it up, then neither do you. Damn, Shannon, where yo' game at?"

"Game? Fuck that game. I love this man. To hell with you. I'ma marry his ass. All I need to know from you is what I have to do to get his sympathy. Make him feel sorry for me, so that I can play on him feeling bad and go in for the kill."

"Well, don't go hog spitin' phlegm. That would fuck your whole situation up. Just lay in the bed and moan, and make sure your coochie is clean."

"What, bitch?"

"Freshen it up and place some Victoria's Secret apple spray between your thighs."

"Why?" she said, surprised.

"So when you get his ass where you want 'im, he can have breakfast on you. Always be prepared."

She laughed. "You should get paid for your ho qualities. They really are outstanding." She hung up.

Taj came back into the bedroom with a towel wrapped around his waist. "I have a twelve hour shift tonight. In between time, when I get a break, I'll stop over at the shop. Do you need anything, before I leave?" he said, removing his towel and then slipping on his boxers.

"Depends on what you're offering."

He smiled. Then he bent over so he and I were face-to-face as I sat on the edge of the bed. He placed his forehead against mine and said, "While I'm out, don't play me. Behave."

"What do you mean *behave*?" Before I could get him to answer, the phone rang.

"Yes, Shannon?" I said, answering the phone.

"It worked, girl! I'm on my way to the emergency room! Hollah!"

I fell out laughing, but Taj didn't seem amused. "What's your problem?" I asked him.

"You."

"What did I do?"

"You're still playing games," he insisted.

"What games?"

"You know what games. That guy Roger keeps calling here, and I peeped the new Movado watch you been rockin'."

"I can't wear a new watch now?" I said, sucking my teeth.

"Movado, Vera?"

"So."

"So? Understand this, check yourself and stop playing with me. I will leave your ass high and fuckin' dry. Believe dat. You're not slick, Vera."

"Taj, I bought this watch."

He chuckled. "Stop runnin' game. You're no good at it. Now, look, let me let you in on a secret. A chick with real game would have taken the watch that she got from Roger back to the store, received a store credit, came and got me, and then we would have picked out a watch together. I would have paid for the watch, then the next day, you would've taken my receipt back to the store, got the money back, purchased the watch with the store credit, and laughed all the way to the bank."

Damn, this mu'fucker is good, I thought to myself. Why didn't I think of that? Instead, the watch Roger sent, I took it back to the Movado store on Madison and exchanged it for the one with the princess cut diamonds completely filling the face.

I rolled my eyes and said, "Taj, please." Then I paused and hit him with the weakest line in the book: "I don't have anything to hide. If I had something to hide, then I would have played you like that."

"Bullshit," he said, playfully mushing me on the side of my head. "You just didn't think of it. But I'm warning you, play me if you want to, and your ass will be in tears."

Psst, this nigga really don't know me. The last time I cried over a man, Old D.B. had dropped out of rehab. Ever since then I'd been straight. I just looked at Taj as if to say, "please," because the real deal was that Roger tried to apologize his way back into my life.

He called begging me to please reconsider our relationship.

"Relationship!" I said to him, nasty and full of venom. "You are such a joke!"

"I understand," Roger said, pleading, but with an edge of coldness. "I get it."

After that I got the watch in the mail with a note that read: *Your time will come.*

As I was going to explain the situation to Taj, I figured fuck him! It seemed that he always thought I was playing a game, so let him think that.

Taj's breath was cool hitting my lips as he spoke. "I told you to tell him once before to stop calling, and he hasn't."

"Taj, please spare me." Then I jumped off the bed, with an attitude and walked toward the bathroom. I felt him watching my ass as I was leaving the room.

"Why did you leave me in the trash dump?" I practiced saying to myself in the bathroom mirror. "Why did you leave me in the trash dump?" Nobody answered.

I cracked the door open and looked into my bedroom to see if Taj had gone. He was already dressed in his mint green scrubs and was hanging his stethoscope around his neck. He dabbed some Dolce &Gabbana behind each ear, ran his tongue over his teeth, and headed toward the bathroom. He didn't bother to knock. He stuck his head into the open crack, where I was standing with no bra and a pair of green silk panties on.

"My father always said to never leave the person you love upset, so I'll just say this, I love you, but don't fuck it up."

I ignored him. Ten minutes later, I came out of the bathroom and noticed that it was only seventy-thirty, but I didn't have plans on going into the shop until nine. I slipped on Taj's favorite Victoria's Secret green apple pushup bra, a pair of beaded Manolo thongs, and a sleeveless DKNY black denim dress, and headed out the door. I jumped in my X5 and slowly drove toward Lincoln Street.

When I called Aunt Cookie to tell her what I wanted to do, she refused to go with me. Instead she said, "Don't get down there and show yo' ass, Vera! Have them talkin' 'bout what Cookie did, what Cookie didn't do. I hate to wreck shop on Lincoln Street! Tell 'em I said don't fuck wit' ya, 'cause Aunt Cookie will beat a mu'fucker down!"

As I slowly rode down Lincoln Street, I saw Rowanda dressed in a pair of jeans, a white T-shirt, and her hair hanging in a long ponytail. She was smacking on a piece of chewing gum and she had her purse draped across her breast. I pulled over to the side of the street and said, "Rowanda! Where you going?"

She walked slowly across the street. I couldn't tell if she actually didn't know it was me, or if she couldn't believe that I had actually come to look for her.

"Vee?" she said, standing at the passenger side of the window.

"Yeah."

"What you doin' here, Vee? You know niggas is gettin' jacked around here, 'specially this early in the morning, and I don't feel like fightin' no mu'fucker for messin' wit' my baby."

"Rowanda, I came to see you."

"Me?"

"Yes."

"Well, I tell you what," she snapped. "If you think I'ma stand here while you cussin' me and tellin' me how I'm a fiend, you dead wrong!"

"I didn't come for that. I came to talk to you."

"About what?" she said, leaning against the door.

"Tell me about my father," I said, surprised at myself. I had no intentions on asking her this.

"Larry Turner?" She frowned.

"He was my father, wasn't he?"

"Yeah, if that's what you wanna call him. Larry wasn't shit. Cookie can tell you that. He ain't give a fuck about nobody but himself."

"Not even me? You had a baby with a man that didn't even give a fuck about me?"

"Vera, I was fifteen years old," she said defensively.

"And that's all you have to say for yourself? So fuckin' what? I was still a child."

"Look, Vee," she said, cutting me off. "I'm sorry, but I don't have no 'white picket fence, Jack and Jill fell in love on the hill, met, married, and then fucked the nigga' story to tell you. I had a hard life, so don't expect no love story. Your Uncle Boy is all the daddy that you need to know."

I swallowed the lump in my throat. "Is Larry Turner the reason you put me in the trash dump?"

"Vee," she said, holding her head down, leaning away from the car and looking at her feet, "I lay in that bed and quivered in pain all night long. I lay there and I was shaken, I was shittin', and I was screaming and hollering *why*! I ain't know what I had done to be born a dog in this life. So, when my back cracked open and you dropped out my pussy like a ball of fire, I wrapped you in a white sheet and figured that you had a better chance in a trash dump than a life in hell with me, and that ain't have nothin' to do wit' Larry Turner."

I couldn't stand to hear any more, so I took off.

The late summer sun was slow about creeping its way into the sky, and seeing that it was covered mostly by gray, I was sure that today would be in slow motion when I arrived at the shop.

DeAndre, my assistant, sat at his station with a cup of Dunkin' Donuts coffee in his hand, mad as hell because he couldn't control the rain. "The weatherman fuckin' with my commission!" he announced as I walked in the door. "Humph, I can't tell Rent-A-Center that their fifty-seven dollars is outside in the rain."

"Rent-A-Center?" I asked.

"That's right! Rent-A-Center is the ghetto's Ethan Allen. You feel me? Their shit is badder than King's Furniture."

"You could always move," the Dominican shampoo girl, Rosa, insisted. "Papi, Rent-A-Center be too high."

"You gonna have to break that down for me," DeAndre said.

"Check this, papi. If you call 'em de day before you move and have dem deliver de stuff, you just jet de next day."

"Mm-hmm, and be picked up that afternoon. Humph, let me try that and I'll have Spiderman on my ass, shootin' webs and blindin' folks, throwin' kryptonite and shit. Naw, I'll pass. That's too ghetto-fab for me!"

"Y'all ever have anything on layaway?" I asked.

"Heck yeah," DeAndre responded. "My mother would layaway a damn man if she could! What about you?"

"Anything I ever had on layaway never came off," I said, flopping down in my station chair. "When my grandma was alive, she would say, "I got y'all something for Christmas, but it's on layaway.""

"Damn, for Christmas?" Rosa asked.

"Hell, yeah, for Christmas. The only thing we could ever count on being there for Christmas was the Charlie Brown special and the Macy's parade. Santa always got jacked before he hit my part of the projects."

"Yeah, you about right," DeAndre said. "One Christmas Eve, when I was ten, my brother came in the house half-drunk with blood on his shirt. When my mother asked him what happened, he told her that he had just shot Rudolph. That shit fucked me up. I thought he was talking about the reindeer, not the kid down the hall. 'Til this day, I still need therapy behind that."

We all fell out laughing.

"When did y'all discover that you actually lived in the ghetto?" DeAndre asked.

"When the heifer went to college!" Shannon said, coming in snacking on a pretzel with three hickeys on her neck.

"How are you just going to get in our conversation?" I said to her as she walked over and gave me a kiss on the cheek. "Anyway," I said, "she's right. And to answer your question, I realized it when mu'fuckas actually paid their gas and electric bill after October fifteenth. That was the first hint!"

They all laughed.

"What about y'all?" I asked.

"Well me," DeAndre said, "I realized that I lived in the ghetto when I started going to college in Long Island and my roommate let this kid talk about his mama and he ain't drop his ass! That's when I knew that somehow shit was different!"

"Hold up," DeAndre said, concentrating on the song that just came on the radio. "Wait a minute now. Rosa," he said, "turn that up, mami!"

The radio sang A Taste of Honey's "Boogie Oogie Oogie." As the band's bass guitar dipped into the beat and the rhythm made its way through the shop, DeAndre set it off with doing a dance called the Slide, and Rosa came up behind him and started breaking it down with a dance called the Bus Stop.

Hold up now. I gotta join this crew! Watch this the robot! Hey-ey!

"Oh, you think you got a move?" DeAndre said as the disc jockey dropped "New York City Girl" over A Taste of Honey's bass guitar. The shit was on and poppin'!

DeAndre grabbed Shannon and they broke out into the Hustle. With all of the music and dancing, nobody noticed when Roger came in and back-slapped me! I fell to the floor before anybody noticed that I was bleeding out the side of my mouth.

"What, you break dancing?" DeAndre asked as he slapped his hand on the floor to do the spin. Then he realized that it wasn't a break dancing contest he was in.

Before I could reclaim my balance, Shannon and DeAndre jumped Roger, and Rosa went in her purse, screaming, "Hold up! I got a knife!"

Roger managed to muscle himself away from Shannon. He pulled out his gun and said, "Back the fuck up!" He came toward me.

The last conversation that I had with Roger raced through my mind as he ran toward me. I had called him a bastard, a cheat, worse than dog shit! And I told him that if I could somehow fix him for the pain that he has probably caused his wife and his children over the years, then I would sock it to 'im! He laughed, but the laughter was cold.

"What the fuck you say the other night, bitch?" Roger said, pointing the gun in my face. "I been tastin' this moment. I been wantin' to fuck yo' ass up! I been breathin' for this," Roger said, now pointing the gun to my head. "Say it, bitch! Say it to my face! I got a good mind to fuckin' kill you! All the time that I have wasted on your silly ass! You'se a dumb bitch! All the effortless nights!"

"Roger, baby," I said, with my voice trembling, "why are you doing this? How can you love me and want to kill me? Please don't do this."

"Baby, please? Now I get a kind word 'cause you're begging for your life. Now you show me some type of affection because I have a gun to your head? You made a fool out of me! You used and played me, and now my wife is gone! Everything that I have had for the last thirty-one years has ended all because I fell in love with you."

My body started to tremble as I said, "I'm so sorry, Roger, but don't kill me, please."

"Kill you?" he said. "Why shouldn't I kill you? Then we would be even."

"What did I do that was so bad?" I cried.

"Shut the fuck up! All I did was try and love you. Anything you needed, I gave it to you! And what did you do? You left me for another nigga. No good-bye, nothing. Do you know how many nights I sat outside your house and watched you carry on with this mu'fucka, rubbing the shit in my face? If I killed your ass, it would serve you fuckin' right."

"Roger, please."

"Roger, please? Vera," he said, shaking his head, "as much as I wanna squeeze the trigger, I can't. I just wanted you to feel at least some of the pain that I feel. I just wanted you to tremble and to ache, so that you could feel what you've done to me!"

Just then Taj and Rowanda walked in together, and I heard Taj telling her, "Just try, Rowanda. She's worth it."

Roger took the gun from my head and quickly brushed past Taj as he left, almost knocking him to the floor.

"What the fuck?" Taj said, looking around. "Vera, what the hell just happened here?"

"Nothing. I'm fine," I said, still shaking.

"He lucky he left when he did!" DeAndre said, looking toward the door. "'Cause in two more minutes, I was gonna drop-kick his ass! Vera, I'm telling you, take it from me, leave that nigga alone! Please. Roger is crazy."

"Leave him alone? Roger is crazy?" Taj said, more to himself than to me. "That was Roger?" he said, pointing over his shoulder. "That was Roger? The same mu'fucka that I told you to leave alone. The same nigga I just spoke to you about this morning? You were still fuckin' with him? Answer me!" Taj stared me in the face. "Don't fuckin' lie either. I swear to God, if you lie to me, I'ma hurt you!"

"No," I cried, "it wasn't like that. Nothing happened. I told him that I—I—" I stuttered, with tears falling from my eyes and sliding between my lips. "I was confused and—"

"Confused?" Taj said, cutting me off. His voice started to tremble. "You weren't fuckin' confused! I kept telling you to stop trying dumb shit, and you didn't listen! I been here, Vera. Me, Taj. I been the one holding, loving, listening, and encouraging you. Being strong for you, being a man for you, and you been fuckin' playin' me? I kept talking to you, and I told you to stop playing with love, because love would turn around and beat yo' ass!

"You are so damn stupid! You act like you fuckin' crazy, always doing a bunch of dumb shit! I am so sick of you and this bullshit. I'm done. This is over! Stay the fuck out of my life!"

Taj turned away from me and walked toward the door. He slammed the door so hard that the glass fell out and shattered all over the floor. I screamed his name for him to come back, but he didn't. All I could hear was the whistle of the wind as it slipped into the crack while the automatic locks clicked.

Stuck

Heartbreak is the worst son of a bitch that you could ever meet. The feel of the heart cracking; the aching of the voice when you wanna say something but can't because your words get lost in the tear-filled memory of how your heart became broken in the first place; the desire to laugh, but having to keep it buried because you don't know if you may holler in joy or bellow out in pain, is some deep shit. Deep enough to keep my ass laying in the bed, dripping tears, holding my chest, and making sure that the crack from the inside doesn't seep all the way through.

I lay in the bed for three days. I hadn't answered the phone, I hadn't gone into the shop, hadn't even eaten. All I did was cry and think, think and cry. I would think about how not to cry, think about why I shouldn't cry, and then think about what else there was to do but cry.

All my life I had contemplated life and how to live it, and I thought that going full speed ahead, hustlin' niggas, playin' married men, while ducking and dodging my heart, was the way to get by. It was the way to get through, because then, I could deal with hating my mother and despising my father. I could feel safe knowing that I had never given my love away to anybody that couldn't take care of it, like Rowanda and Larry, but Taj was different. I needed him, I loved him, and I was not afraid anymore to let the world know that I was so in love with this man that I didn't even know how to describe what I was feeling inside. The separation was killing me.

The first day I decided to get out of bed and check the mail, it rained. The rain beat against the windowpane and ran down the glass like lost souls looking for an end. I walked back into the foyer and into the kitchen, and when I threw the mail on the center island, it slid on the floor and I left it there.

I had dialed Taj's phone number a hundred times over and over again, only to hang up before the first ring or before I pressed the last number. I kept looking at his picture and running my fingers across the image, as if I could taste him. I could still feel his touch melting into my skin, and I could still remember the look on his face when he said, "It's over!"

Tears welled up in my throat and fell from the corners of my eyes. I placed my head down on my kitchen island and cried into the fold of my arm.

"That mu'fucka is a piece of work, ain't he?" Shannon said, scaring me. I jumped up and wiped my eyes.

"How did you get in here? And what mu'fucka?"

"I have a key, remember? And the mu'fucka is better known as love. That nigga is a bitch, ain't he? And he's selfish. He just moves right in, takes up residence, and never once does he get your permission. And if you don't recognize his ass when he arrives, you damn sure know the nigga by the time he leaves."

"Amen to that," I said, wiping my eyes, which were now burning from holding back tears. Just then I noticed that Shannon had her Louie V. duffle bag and her makeup case.

"What, are you moving in?" I asked.

"Yep, for now anyway. It was decided over a conference call."

"A conference call?"

"Yes, one of our get-'im-girl sessions. Me, Angie, and Lee unanimously agreed that I was the only one who could tolerate your mouth long enough to spend long and extended periods of time with you. Plus," she said, dropping her bags in the middle of the floor and then opening the refrigerator and taking out a pack of chicken, "I need my hair done, and you're my hairstylist."

I shot her ass a look.

"Don't be looking at me like that," she said, frowning up her face. "Plus, we need to talk."

"About what?" I said.

"About you and how you got to slow your ass down before you be out in the cold. I don't know about you, but the next time I get pregnant, not only am I keeping my baby, but the man that I'm pregnant by will be my husband. Furthermore, you my girl and all, but when I get my husband, I won't be hanging around no horny-ass single women. You got to be fat and frilly."

I started laughing. "You so stupid. Fat and frilly? Never that. But voluptuous? Now, that's more like it. Plus, I ain't the one you have to watch out for. You better look out for Angie's sneaky ass, or Lee. Yeah, Lee, that'll be the one to getcha."

Shannon laughed. "I'll fuck her ass up, but don't be changing the subject. Lee is not the issue. Lee's shit has passed, now it's your turn. We'll talk. Just give me a few minutes to freshen up."

"Freshen up?" I said. "You just walked in the door."

"For your information," she said with a smirk, "I had some dick before I came over here—and not the shit that you buy at the nasty-girl store. I had some fresh dick. Okay? So, like I said, give me a minute. I need to freshen up."

I couldn't help but laugh.

"But in the meantime, here," Shannon said, handing me the pack of chicken and fresh vegetables. "I'm hungry. Cook me something to eat while I shower and change my clothes."

"Are you serious? Cook? And eat? I don't have an appetite."

"Well, goddamn! You real fucked up. Now, Vera, tell me, ain't it somethin' when the script flip and you on the outside looking in? Begging and pleading for love to come back? Girl, please. Love's ass know he da bomb!" Then she smiled and went up the stairs.

I grilled the chicken and steamed the vegetables. For a little pizza, I sprinkled some curry in the vegetables and steamed some butterfly shrimp as a topping. I toasted a roll of French garlic bread, and when I was done, what I had in front of me was Taj's favorite meal. And then, suddenly it was as if an internal thunderstorm had occurred and lightning began to strike. I broke down and cried.

Shannon came downstairs dressed in olive green silk pajamas. "Come here, girl," she said, holding her arms out. "You got to stop acting like this. Crying is not going to bring him back."

I placed my head on her shoulder and said, "I didn't know that I could love him like this. He was supposed to be a fling, that's it. I was never supposed to fall in love."

"Vera," Shannon said, "let's sit down, 'cause I need to eat while we talk."

She fixed our plates, and we sat at the kitchen table. "Girlfriend, love is full time and sometimes overtime, but it is never, ever part time. You cannot turn it on and off when you're not in the mood."

"But I was starting to be in the mood."

"Girl, please. Yo' ass was already there. Listen, I understand that you have your issues with Rowanda, but it's like that shit effects everything that you do. Deal with that shit. Deal with Rowanda. That's your mother and she's not going anywhere. If she has hurt you and you want to know why she left, why she couldn't be there for you, why she couldn't be your mother, and how come she had to always get high. If that's what you want to know, then ask. Put it out there and then leave it."

"It's not just Rowanda," I said, making an effort to eat a piece of shrimp.

"What else is it? Your father, Larry Turner? Girl, write his ass a letter and then burn it up. But before you burn it, step to his ass and tell him how you feel. Tell Larry that you're pissed the fuck off that he was never your father. Tell his ass that you can't seem to settle with love because you keep wrestling with him and Rowanda. Keep a journal, write a letter, do something, and then take a pen and cuss their asses out! 'Cause this here, the shit you're doing to yourself, has to end, because Taj is not going to wait forever."

"Obviously," I said. "He's not here."

"He's not here," Shannon said, "because you fucked up, plain and simple."

"But what if I go and he doesn't want to be bothered with me? You heard him when he said it's over. Fuck that. I'm not the type to be beggin' no man."

"Beggin'? What the fuck? Drop that false-ass pride and go get that nigga. You all up in here crying and shit, can't eat, can't sleep, don't know whether you comin' or going. Chile, spare me. This is Shannon you're talking to, and I know yo' ass like a book. That man loves you, probably more than you love yourself, and nothing is worth losing a good man, especially not yo' fake-ass pride."

"Shannon, please."

"Shannon, please? Do you know how hard it is to find a good brotha that's not gay, incarcerated, on the down low, married, dead, or confused? Girlfriend, please. That's exactly why, when I went through my shit with Quincy, I checked myself, learned from my mistakes, and moved on. Now, my man is at home watching TV, waiting on me, and as long as he's good to me, has good credit and a job, then we can have something. So, needless to say, I got mine. Now you got to get yours."

"Shannon," I said, as if I were exhausted, "I am so confused with this shit. It's like, how can I love this man and how can this man love me, knowing that my mother is a fuckin' drug addict? How is he so in love with me when I can't even deal with my past?"

"It's your past, Vera. It's not your future. And your mother is on drugs, not you. Stop dealing with her drug habit. Deal with yourself. You're taking too much responsibility for her. Let some of that shit go, and go get that man. I'm telling you, the clean up woman gonna snatch him up, and you will be out in the cold."

"And what if he doesn't want to be bothered?"

"That's a chance you have to take, but I doubt it. And guess what? If he doesn't want to be bothered, then you take your heartache and step. Then, all that could mean is he wasn't supposed to be your man. He was supposed to be your lesson, and the next time you get a good man, you'll know how to treat him. But from the way I see it, if you play your cards right, you and Taj should be fuckin' by this time tomorrow night."

I chuckled slightly, looked at her, and said, "Well, I'll think about it."

"That's on you," she said, stuffing a piece of shrimp in her mouth. "Like I said, my man laying in the bed waiting on me."

I bit the inside of my lip and held back as many tears as I could. Then I got up, ran upstairs, and went into the bathroom and hopped in the shower. I got dressed in my low rise J-Lo jeans with the black leather patches on the front and the faded denim on the back. I slipped on my black leather tube top, my Jimmy Choos, and was fierce on my way out the door.

"Where are you going?" Shannon asked as I came down the stairs.

"I'm going to get my man," I said.

"That's what's up!" She smiled.

Step Nine

I stood and stared at the bells outside of the building Taj lived in for at least fifteen minutes before I thought about pressing the buzzer. It had started raining again, and people were staring at me as I stood motionless, with raindrops covering my skin.

"Looking for someone?" a voice from over my shoulder said. I turned around and saw Taj. He was dressed in his scrubs and looked as if he had just come from work.

"I was in the neighborhood, so, you know."

"No, I don't know," he said as he turned the key into the door. "But look, I just worked a double shift. I gotta go."

"Taj, I . . ."

"Go home, Vera. I have things to do." He slammed the door in my face.

I cried all the way to my truck. I cried so much that when I started driving, I had to pull over to the side of the road and scream. I beat my hands against the dashboard and screamed in agony. I held my head down and cried into the steering wheel.

As soon as I placed my hands over my burning eyes, I heard a tap on the window and then I heard a muffled voice say, "Open the door, Vera."

I looked up at Taj. "Open the door," he said again. I shook my head.

"Open the door, Vera."

I wiped my eyes and shook my head again.

"Open the goddamn door, Vera!"

I opened the door, and he gently lifted me out of my truck. I wrapped my arms around his neck and my legs around his waist. He placed his hands underneath my butt, and he placed me against my truck's door, with my back resting on the glass. The heavy rain dripped in slow motion as the night sky unzipped Heaven's tears and it began to drench our clothes. I placed my head on his shoulder and inhaled the scent of his body.

"Hold your head up and look at me," he said.

I held my head up, but I didn't unwrap my legs or my arms. He locked his arms under my butt, and his grip was strong. "Do you love me?" he asked.

I nodded my head.

"No, say it to me," he said. "And look at me when you say it."

"I love you," I said, while licking the salty tears away from my lips.

"Then why you keep fuckin' up?"

"I don't mean to, but look, Taj," I said, taking a deep breath. "All I know is that I'm in love with you. I can't lose you, and I swear nothing happened between Roger and me. Nothing."

"Yeah?" he said with a frown.

"My right hand to God, baby. Nobody in this world is worth losing you for. I never knew that I could love someone as much as I love you. I can't let you go. I'm not letting you go. Whatever you need, I got it."

"All I want is your heart."

Tears started rolling down my cheeks. He kissed my tears away and he said, "Do you know how many times I thought about leaving and staying gone? Girl, I am so in love with you to the point where I can't even think straight. But I won't tolerate being played, because I'm not into that bullshit. Now, if you wanna be with me, then it's all or nothing."

"Everything is yours," I said. "Just give me another chance."

"Then treat me like I should be treated," he said. "Stop shutting me out. Love me. Let me hold you. Let me be there for you. Allow me to be your man. When you want to talk about Larry

Turner or Rowanda, come to me. That's why I'm here. Talk to me, don't hold it in. Tell me your problems, and I will do what I can to solve them."

"I have to solve my own problems."

"But I can lead you to the solutions."

"I love you so much, Taj."

"Actions speak louder than words. Show me that you love me. I'm your man and that's it. Now, either you treat me like that, or I'm gone. No more two and three chances. I'm done with that shit. This is it. It's all or nothing, and I will only settle for everything."

"All I can give you is my heart," I said.

"That's all I need."

I hugged him so tight that I ended up melting into his embrace. I never wanted to let him go.

He gently placed me on the ground, kissed me passionately while stroking my back, and somehow, in between the hissing breeze and the rhythm of the rain drops, we began to grind slowly, and somehow we ended up lost in the rhythm of one another's heartbeat.

Step Ten

By now, you would think that I felt safe, but I didn't. I was scared. Taj had my heart, and no matter what plans my mind made, my heart beat them out hands down, and here I was, ironically at the mercy of Taj's love.

It had started to get a little cold, even though it was only the beginning of September.

"Get up. Let's go for a ride," Taj said. I wasn't the least bit surprised, but I was exhausted. We had been up all night talking.

"What are you going to do about Rowanda?" he asked, while slipping on his beige velour Sean John sweat suit.

"Nothing."

"And you think that you can live the rest of your life doing nothing about your mother?"

"Perhaps," I said extra snappy, letting him know that I didn't want to hear the shit! I was in love with him, yes, but the situation with Rowanda was not to be touched. "Plus, I don't wanna talk about it."

"You need to stop that."

"Stop what?"

"Stop being so stubborn."

"I'm not being stubborn. I just don't want to hear about it. Didn't you just say let's go for a ride? Well, let's do that!"

"Okay. Okay," he said, throwing both his hands in the air, looking sexier than ever.

He went to grab his Coach leather paperboy knapsack, but I was already close and practically in his chest by the time he went to reach over to the dresser. I placed my head on his chest and hugged him around his waist. I almost wanted to cry, but I got it together and instead, held him close. I could feel with the tightening of his embrace that he understood.

"It's all right, baby," he said into my double-strand twist that I had twisted into a French roll. "It's all right."

When we got into Taj's Escalade, I could almost lose myself in the softness of the black leather seats. The sound of Will Downing's "A Million Ways to Please a Woman" was filtering throughout the speakers, and it was so crisp and so clear that I felt like Will Downing was sitting next to me.

"This is a nice CD," I said to Taj with my eyes closed.

"Yeah, it is. I listen to it on my way home a lot of times. It relaxes me. Makes me think about you."

I started blushing. "Jonathan Butler has a nice CD as well," I said.

"Jonathan Butler?" he said, as if he were impressed.

"Yes, Jonathan Butler. What, all you think I listen to is Jay-Z and Lil John?"

"I never said that. Maybe not Lil John. More like Lil' Kim."

"Whatever."

"I'm playing, baby." He laughed. "But look, do you know that the type of music a person listens to speaks volumes about their personality?"

"Really? And how do you figure that?"

"Because if all you listen to is hardcore gansta rap or heavy metal music, then that usually means that your world is somehow surrounded with what they are talking about. Otherwise, why you want to hear about bitches suckin' dick, niggers gettin' hit, and somebody killing their mama fifty times a day?"

"You have a slight point, but I happen to like rap."

"Me too, but that's not all I listen to."

"Well, my favorite is jazz," I said.

"Jazz?" he asked, surprised. "Something I didn't know about my baby, huh?

"That's right, jazz. See, you learn something new every day."

"What do you know about jazz, besides Mr. Will? Do you know anything about the real deal? Like Coltrane, Holiday, Davis, Parker? What do you really know about jazz?"

"Excuse you, boyfriend, but I do know that jazz is the only original American art form when it comes to music. And not only do I have the CDs by the legends you just named, but I also have a few by Lionel Hamilton, Sarah Vaughn, Nina Simone, and that's just to name a few, so don't sleep."

"Don't sleep? You're something else. So, tell me, Miss Jazz Lady, how long have you wanted to be a hairstylist?"

"Since I was a little girl. Rowanda used to dream it all the time, so I just felt it was something I needed to become."

"My mother died when I was twelve, and I always said if I were a doctor, I could've saved her."

"Oh," I said. I felt a little awkward commenting on that, so I left it alone.

As we headed through the Holland Tunnel, I felt a little sleepy, so I got lost in the world of

Will Downing's music and drifted off for a short nap.

When I opened my eyes, Taj was rubbing my face and saying, "We're here, baby."

"Where are we?"

"South Fourteenth Street."

"Jerscy?"

"Not just Jersey, Newark, baby girl. Brick City! My family lives in the red house on the corner."

When I stepped out of the truck, I noticed instantly that the ghetto has a universal beauty no matter where you go, no matter what river you cross, no matter what train you take. It always has the same tune, the same beat, the same rhythm of the Puerto Rican corner store, the famous Madison Lounge with the storefront Laundromat, and black people everywhere of all shapes and sizes, some singing a poverty tune, some signing a home tune, and some singing a tune with a where-else-is-there-to-go flavor. People all over feel a connection with their ghetto segment of the world, and it's all love, it's all good, no matter what hood your ghetto is derived from.

So, I understood when Taj's father, who looked identical to his son, was eating a bowl of grits and sitting on the stoop trying to play dominos, and Taj's brother was kickin' it with his boys. I could relate to the fiend on the corner, and the middle-aged lady that seemed to be taking up some of Taj's father's attention. They were one of many in every neighborhood.

"Hey, Pop!" Taj said, giving his father a man-to-man hug and a kiss on the cheek. "What's up?"

"You, babyboy! How you been?"

Before Taj could respond, his brother, who bore a strong resemblance to Taj but seemed to be a few years younger, jumped off the crate he was sitting on and gave his brother a pound and then a hug.

"What's up, man!" Taj said. "I thought you were in Hampton for school?

"I transferred to Rutgers, downtown. I wanted to be closer to home. I started missing y'all, man."

"All right, as long as you're still in school. Political science, right?"

"Yeah, man," Taj's brother said. "Political science."

A little girl, about five or six years old, came running out the door and hugged Taj around his knees. "Uncle Taj! Uncle Taj!"

He squeezed her tight and picked her up. "Tae-Tae, do you see this lady over here?"

"Yes," she said, blushing.

"She's pretty, right?'

"Mm-hmm," Taj's father answered for her.

Taj blushed and said, "This is Vera, everybody. And Vera, this is everybody."

"Humph," Taj's father said, giving me a hug. "Boy, you sure got your daddy's taste. You better be lucky you're my son, otherwise you'd be going home alone."

Taj laughed. "It won't be the first time, Pop. You see you stole Ms. Betty from me," Taj said, pointing to the lady sitting on the stoop with Taj's father.

"Hold on, now," Ms. Betty said. "It ain't like it's too late to get me back!"

"Y'all got issues!" Taj's brother laughed. They all laughed and seemed to be enjoying each other's company.

"Come on in the house," Taj's father said. When he got up, I saw that he had a shirt that said *Rest In Peace Bundles*. Out of curiosity, I asked, "Mr. Bennett, who was Bundles?"

"Oh, baby, he was one of the neighborhood kids that got shot a couple of years back. He grew up with my boys, Taj and Sharief."

"Yeah," Taj said. "I told you about him. Big Stuff. It's the same person."

When I walked into Mr. Bennett's house, there was a young lady sitting on the couch. She was quite pretty, but she also seemed rather young.

"Baby," Taj said, "this is my sister, Samira. My niece's mother." She stood up, and I noticed that she was quite short, no more than five foot three. She had blond-colored box braids in her hair, and her skin was a honey-colored complexion. She resembled Taj slightly.

"How are you? I've heard a lot about you," she said.

"Really?" I said, surprised.

"Mm-hmm. My father doesn't keep any secrets, no matter what my brother thinks. Soon as Taj called and told Daddy that he had found the one, Daddy was right in here telling us every bit of the conversation."

The one? I thought. *Did Taj really say that?* He didn't seem to flinch when his sister said that. Neither did he seem the least bit embarrassed, although what came out of his mouth was, "You talk sooo much, Samira." It didn't seem that he meant that. Instead, it seemed that he felt relieved that somebody had finally lay it on the line.

"I'm glad that he told your father that," I said. "It's wonderful when the feeling is mutual."

"Did you get it?" I asked.

"Did I get it? I had no choice. Pops wasn't playing that, and I was the oldest, too. I had to be the one to set the example. Sharief and Samira were young when my mother died."

"How old were they?"

"Five years old."

"Oh, so how did that make you feel, when your mother died?" I asked Taj, sitting on his old twin-sized bed with the Papa Smurf sheets.

"I felt guilty."

"Why?"

"Because I wanted to save her, but I couldn't."

"What did she die from?"

"Breast cancer."

"How could you have saved her?"

"Because if I had been a doctor, I may have been able to make a difference."

"Baby, you were a little boy."

"I know, but I felt like I should've been a grown man."

I could tell that Taj was starting to get choked up, but he was trying to fight it off, so I changed the subject. "I didn't know you told your father about me. When did you do that?"

"When I first laid eyes on you."

"Are you serious?"

"Quite."

"So, how's it going at the hospital, son?" Taj's father asked, sitting at the 50s-style round kitchen table and smiling at me.

"It's all right, Pop. A lot of long hours."

"Yeah, it's rough out there. I read in the paper there's a doctor shortage."

"Not really," Taj said. "More of a nurse shortage."

"What you do for a living, baby?" Ms. Betty asked, obviously trying to be slick.

Before I answered the question, I gave her a brief overview. She was a cocoa complexion, more like Hershey's chocolate than any other brand. She had auburn-colored hair that wasn't the best match to her skin tone, but it would do. She had a black woman's size eighteen hips, and a Southern girl's twang to her voice. She was standing at the stove, pouring herself a bowl of grits and waiting for a direct answer from me.

Instead of telling her that I was just a hairstylist, I figured I would give her the whole kit and caboodle. "I own a full service hair and nail salon on the corner of Thirty-third and Park in Manhattan. It's mostly for black men and women, although we do get a few whites and Latinos. I have prices that are more down to earth than the other salons in the surrounding area, which is why most of my customers will travel from Brooklyn, Queens, and other places to come and get hooked up at Vera's Hair Creation."

"Humph, a hairstylist with her own salon. I'm impressed, and darlin', you being able to do hair is right up my alley. I been wanting to try those—wait a minute," she said, stepping away from the stove and peeking down the hallway toward the living room. "Samira, what is those things I wanna try?"

"Flat twist, Ms. Betty," Samira answered, seeming somewhat annoyed, as if she had heard that question hundreds of times before.

"Yeah," Ms. Betty said, resuming the conversation. "Flat twist. I been wantin' to try them things, but I been scared they gonna pull my hair out."

"They won't pull your hair out as long as you don't try combing it out."

"What about that gel?"

"Well, I use a little gel because that's what makes the flat twist stay together, but you have to sit under the dryer."

"Oh, one of them bouffant dryers? I got one of them, chile. Right in the other room."

"Okay. Well, I would recommend you going to a salon and getting it done. Not unless you know someone who can do your hair and knows what they're doing."

"My new daughter-in-law."

"Oh," I said to Taj. "Your brother's married?"

He shot me a look like, *Please, you have just opened a can of worms for yourself.* Then I realized it was me she was talking about.

"Oh, me," I said, pointing to my chest. "I don't travel with my hair supplies, Ms. Betty. I'm sorry."

"Chile, there is a Mi-Mi's on just about every corner, with all the hair products you can imagine."

I really was outdone with Ms. Betty's forwardness. Taj seemed a little annoyed, but I could tell that I was under tight scrutiny about the way I was to handle Ms. Betty. She seemed to mean a lot to this entire family, especially since their mother had died, so I was sure that I needed to be careful how I said "I don't think so" to Ms. Betty.

Just when the "I" came out, I completed the sentence with, "can do it. I'll do it."

"Here you go," Taj said, handing me the keys to his Escalade.

"Taj, I don't know where I'm going."

"I know, baby. Don't you see Ms. Betty? Ms. Betty loves to ride."

"Sho' do," Ms. Betty said. "I'll show you where it's at. There's one right on Bergen Street."

Ms. Betty reminded me of Aunt Cookie, but with a little more ghetto poise. She was slick, where Aunt Cookie lay it all on the line. I was certain that if these two met, they wouldn't like each other. Aunt Cookie didn't care for women she thought always had an underlying meaning to anything they said.

When we drove down Clinton Place and cut over a side street to hit Bergen, I answered all of Ms. Betty's questions with a yes or no, including the one she asked about Taj and me living together. She was nosy as hell, and from what I could tell, she was nosy on an ongoing basis.

"How long have you and Mr. Bennett been together?" I asked, right after she had grilled me with the same question.

"For thirty-five years really. Off and on, but after his wife died, we got together all the way."

"All the way?" I said, giving her the same, *Yes, I'm all in your business* look that she was giving to me. "That's interesting," I said, but I was thinking, *You're an old-ass ho, Betty. Taj is only thirty-two.*

"I know what you're thinking," she insisted, "but things happen."

"Oh, Ms. Betty, I understand." *That you was creeping with Viola Bennett's man. Oh, I understand quite well.*

When we arrived at the beauty supply place, it wasn't much different than the ones in New York. All the people in there were Chinese, with the exception of the fake-ass black security guard standing at the door.

When Ms. Betty and I returned, Taj, his father, and his brother were sitting at the kitchen table playing a game of Spades.

"My book!" Taj's brother yelled when I walked in the kitchen and placed my hand on Taj's shoulder. Taj then tilted his head to the side and kissed my hand.

"You get what you needed, baby?"

"Yeah."

"Come on, Vera!" Ms. Betty yelled, excited. "Let's get this started!"

I could feel Taj watching me as I washed Ms. Betty's hair, like he was thinking about when we first met. When I looked over my shoulder, Taj was peeking over his hand of cards and staring at me with a serious look—not one of anger, more like one of appreciation and love. In an effort to break the monotony of the stare, I winked my eye. He winked back and returned to his card game by saying, "Y'all know whoever has the deuce of spades gets the kitty! Don't even try it."

For once in my life, at that very moment, I felt loved—and not just loved, but I felt in love. Here was a man that cared about how I felt, what I thought, the simple things that I had always longed for. There he sat at the kitchen table with his father and brother, laughing and joking, dealing out cards, and making me feel like the queen of hearts, all at the same time.

Miss Betty's hair needed a touch-up like you wouldn't believe, but she wouldn't hear of it. I tried to explain to her that the flat twist were not going to last for a long time as long as her roots were hit, but she wouldn't hear of it.

"My girlfriend Maxine does my relaxers."

"I understand that, Ms. Betty, but your roots really need to be touched up."

"Vera," Taj's sister Samira said, with her daughter Tae-Tae sitting between her legs, "don't argue with Ms. Betty. She has to learn the hard way."

"This is my head!" Ms. Betty snapped at Samira. She snapped more like this was an old and ongoing argument, and not one that just started over a flip comment.

"It's okay, Samira. You're right, Ms. Betty. I'll do my best."

When I was done, Ms. Betty had flat twists going around in a circle all over her head, and a blonde ponytail (at her insistence) swinging on the side. Ghetto fabulous is what she requested. She wanted to be old and young at the same time, and although I hooked up her hair and she was wearing the hell outta this hairstyle, she still resembled an old-ass Shanaynay.

"You got it goin' on, Miss Betty!" Taj said. "My baby certainly hooked you up!"

Quite frankly, I was embarrassed, as this was not my best work. Had she allowed me to choose a style for her, I probably would have given her three goddess braids or twisted her hair into a bun.

"Baby," Taj said, tight-lipped as Ms. Betty walked over to show off her hair to Mr. Bennett, "what the hell did you do to Ms. Betty's hair? I've never seen you do a hairstyle like that."

"That's what she wanted," I responded, tight-lipped. "What was I supposed to do?"

"I don't know, baby, but as soon as Ms. Betty step foot on Fabyan and Hawthorne, I'ma have to get Sharief or Samira to defend you, because all the people headed up to Valley Fair will be asking who in the hell left the gate open!"

I playfully mushed him on the side of his head.

"Give me a kiss," he said.

"Taj, we are sitting at your father's dinner table."

"Just give me a little one, please. They're not looking. Pop too busy lying to Ms. Betty."

I slid him a quick brush against the lips. I saw Ms. Betty peek, but this time, she didn't say anything.

"Come on, baby," Ms. Betty said to me. "Let's leave them in here. Let's go in the living room and talk."

Ms. Betty, Taj's sister, and I talked about everything. I found out that Ms. Betty was never able to have any children, so when Taj's mother died, she stepped in and was able to love Taj and the twins like her own. Although she and Samira didn't seem to always get along, you could tell that they loved one another.

Samira told me that she had recently enrolled in cosmetology school and that her dream was to own her own salon as well. I gave her my card and told that when she graduated she should let me know and she could come work for me. That is, if she didn't mind working in the city.

Ms. Betty told me how much she loved Taj and that she was happy that he found someone who loved him the way that I did.

Once it started to get late, Taj was ready to go home. Ms. Betty insisted that we spend the night. "I know y'all ain't gonna be driving back over to the city in the dark. Come on and stay."

"We can't, Ms. Betty," Taj insisted and kissed her on the cheek. "I'm glad we all had a good time, but I have a long shift tomorrow, so I need to get home."

"And where is home?" Ms. Betty asked, real slick, as if she actually wanted to know the street address, as opposed to who he shared a bed with.

"Avenue K in Brooklyn," I said, more to him than to her.

He smiled and said more to me than to her, "Yes, Avenue K."

"And who lives there?" she asked.

"I lived there first," I explained to her. "Now Taj and I live there together."

"Oh, yeah," she said, sounding relieved, as if her nosy-ass quest to knowing whether or not we lived together was finally conquered, not knowing that it was only at this very moment it was made official.

When we left, everybody promised that the next time, they would come to Brooklyn and visit us.

At first, I thought that sex could never express the way that I felt for this man, my man, Taj, and then I realized that there could never be enough words to describe how he made me feel and how special his whole existence was to me. We lay in the king-sized sleigh bed that was now ours, and our naked bodies were covered by the streams and strips of the moonlight that were sneaking in through the mini blinds. *Was I doing the right thing?* I thought as I took his right hand and placed it on my left breast, so he could feel my heart beating. When he took his lips and pulled the nipple soft, but with a firm grip, I knew that this was it, and this was where I wanted to be.

When we finished making love, I said to Taj, "Tell me about your mother."

"My mother?" he asked, genuinely shocked.

"Yes. Tell me about her."

"My mother was a lot like you. She was rough around the edges, but had silk for the core."

"Really?"

"Yes." He chucked, as if his mind had stumbled upon a memory. "And she could cuss like a sailor!" At this point, he was completely laughing at his own thought. "One time, she cussed Ms. Betty out so bad for sneaking around with my father that Ms. Betty sat at the Madison Lounge for a night straight and drank five rounds of rum. And then, when Ms. Betty stumbled out the bar, Mommy beat her ass!"

"How'd that make you feel?"

"Excuse me?" he said, like he expected me to laugh instead of asking a question. "What is this, flip the script? I can remember having this conversation with you a couple of months ago, except you were on the other side."

I smiled, but gave him a look to let him know that I expected an answer to my question.

"All right, baby. For a long time, I was resentful of Ms. Betty and my father, as well, but I had no one but my father. The twins were small, so they didn't understand. But me, I was old enough to know that Ms. Betty wasn't some nice lady who just wanted to be around. She wanted to take my mother's place."

"Is that how you still feel?"

"Hell, no!" he said, losing control over his tone. "I'm sorry, baby. It's just that sometimes, I can't stand to think of my mother not being here to see me, the twins, my niece, and not being here to meet you, Vera." He turned over and lay on top of me, not in the position of wanting to make love, but more in the position of getting me to listen.

"You have to stop hating Rowanda," he said.

I went to say something, but he placed his finger on my lips. "Let me talk. You only get one mother, and then there's no second chance, believe me. All the memories and dreams that you have of her will not bring her back when she's gone. That'll be it, and you'll find yourself talking to yourself and wishing she were here. Believe me, baby, it's not easy."

He lay his head on my breast, and I wrapped my arms around him, and he nestled in my breast. I could feel the cold wetness of a tear trickling down and running over my nipple.

Step Eleven

"So, you think you wanna be wit' him forever?" Rowanda asked, walking slowly into the shop, looking around.

At first I didn't say anything. I figured what she was asking was really none of her business, but then again, she was trying. "Do I wanna be with who?"

"Taj." She laughed. "Cookie tells me that he keeps you in check, Vee!" When she noticed that I didn't think the shit was cute, she tilted her head down and walked toward me. "May I give you a kiss on the cheek?"

"For what?"

"Because I haven't been able to laugh with you since you were seven years old and the drunk old lady was riding a kid's bike and kept hitting the curb."

The thought of that instantly made me smile. To see the drunk old lady riding a Hot Wheels in front of the projects, hittin' the curb and cussin' at folks, saying, "What y'all motherfuckas lookin' at?"

All of a sudden, I was stretched out in laughter, and I reminded Rowanda of how the old lady said, "I will bust a nigga's ass that fuck wit' me and my ride!"

Rowanda laughed so hard that she cried. "And do you remember when she hit the curb and tilted to the side? She hit a wheelie and started signing the Dramatics' version of 'Outside In the Rain'?" Rowanda laughed so hard you would have thought that she was bellied over in pain.

Once I wiped the tears from my eyes, I noticed how Rowanda was staring at me, how she stroked my double strand twist, and began to play in my hair. "Remember how I used to do your hair? Remember when I told you that I wanted you to be a beautician?"

"A hairstylist, Rowanda," I said, quickly correcting her. "A beautician stands in the kitchen with a straightening comb and a hot plate, but a hairstylist is runnin' the show."

"All right, all right. A hairstylist."

"Yes, I remember."

"I was so proud of you when Cookie told me that you graduated from college and you had a cosmetology degree. I was never happier. When Cookie told me that you opened your shop, I used to sit across the street on the bench and watch you sometimes in the morning."

"You did that? Why?"

"Because you're my baby. I'm your mother, and I love you."

"I don't wanna talk about that."

"Talk about what?" she asked.

"About being your baby and you being my mother. I'm not ready to deal with that."

She didn't say anything. She stood still for a moment and then said, "What time you closing?"

"The shop is already closed. That's why nobody's here. Why?"

"I wanted to spend some time with you."

"For what? We just spent time."

She made a swallowing motion with her throat. "I don't wanna let go of the laughter."

"We can't pretend that you been clean all my life, and I will not fake the funk that I wasn't left in a trash dump to make you feel better."

"You don't have the ability to make me feel good or bad. That's for God to do."

"Well, that may be so, but I'm just letting you know."

"Well, let me know on the way home," she said.

"Home?"

"Yes. Lincoln Street."

When I parked in front of the building that Rowanda called home, I noticed that the buildings weren't as big as they seemed when I was child. I got out and looked around like a stranger in my own homeland, desperately trying to search for the feeling that I had the night before social services took me away.

Rowanda grabbed my hand and squeezed. I squeezed back and smiled. When we stepped in the courtyard, I appreciated the beauty of the projects.

Lincoln Street was lined with buildings from one corner to the next, and they all seemed to get along. The music in the courtyard was a DJ mix of dopefiends, welfare queens, some tryin' to make it, and some who just couldn't take it. But the commonality was "the struggle," and that was what made 'em laugh, made 'em cry, made 'em die, and made 'em stay alive, and hold on tight to a building filled with untold stories, dreams, and life lessons.

Dirty and Biggie were outside in front building 251A, sitting in their ride, throwing up gang signs and listening to Fifty Cent's "Gangsta."

Rowanda's attitude instantly changed as she walked over to the driver's side of the custom made Coupe Deville convertible and slapped the shit out of Dirty in the back of his head.

"I told y'all niggas 'bout that shit! Don't be bringing that gang shit 'round here!" The way she gave 'em that Aunt Cookie look, they knew she wasn't playing. For the first time in my life, I could see that Rowanda was strong, and it didn't take much to set her off. "Show some respect. You see Vee standin' here!"

"What up, cuz?" Dirty said. Biggie just nodded his head. "Get y'all asses out the car and come upstairs! Vee gonna stay a li'l while," Rowanda said, ghetto as hell, sounding like the twin version to Wanda Sykes, with her hands on her hips and her mouth tooted up, reminding me of myself.

"A'ight, Ro, damn," Dirty said, snatching his car radio out of the socket.

"And don't be cussin', either."

I was a little taken aback by Rowanda and how she handled Dirty and Biggie like she was their mother, and not her twin, Towanda. Towanda was a nasty bitch, and nobody liked her. She got high off of everything from baby aspirin to angel dust. Towanda stayed around Lincoln Street for a little while, but she got the full pledge package and couldn't afford the cocktail. Took her three months to die, leaving Dirty and Biggie with Grandma, Rowanda, and me.

The apartment wasn't as empty as I last remembered. There was some furniture now: a futon, a table, some magazines, and a baby picture of me. The kitchen and the living room shared the same space. The small square wooden table was spotless, and it sat next to the small gas stove that contained half of Rowanda's beauty in the pilot. The refrigerator was olive green, with rust spots underneath the silver handles. The kitchen wall behind the stove had old grease spots, and some of the tile on the floor was missing in various spaces, but the apartment had improved. Somebody could call it home now, and there was no more echo to reflect the emptiness.

Biggie and Dirty flopped down on the futon and began to talk with Rowanda. It became evident that their lives had gone on without me, and that bothered me.

"I see y'all been livin'," I said with a smirk.

"Who?" Rowanda asked, taking food out of the refrigerator. "We makin' it a little. Dirty and Biggie think I'm stupid. They think I don't know they still slingin' that shit, but if I find it under that futon again, I'ma flush it in the toilet!"

"Ro, don't be flushin' my shit!" Dirty jerked his head and said, "Leave that shit alone. How else we gonna eat?"

"I'm gonna get a job."

"Well, until you get one, I'ma continue my quest in pleasing the neighborhood."

"Pleasing the neighborhood?" I said with an attitude. "You fuckin' it up! Nobody around here will get out of the slump they in if you keep dealing that shit."

"Hey, I ain't make 'em get high," Dirty said. "By the time I was born, most of them were already gettin' on."

"Whatever." I was beginning to feel uneasy, but I wanted to stay.

My cell phone started ringing as I went to talk to Rowanda. It was Taj on the line.

"Hey, baby!" I said, excited.

"Hey, baby!" he replied, just as excited. "Where are you?" he asked.

"On Lincoln Street."

"Lincoln Street?"

"Yeah. It's a long story."

"Do you need me?"

"Yes, but not now."

I could tell he was smiling. "Tell me you love me, Vera."

"I got one better," I said. "I more than just love you. I'm madly in love with you."

"That's what's up, baby. That's what's up."

Rowanda was watching me dead in my mouth

when I was on the phone with Taj. "I guess that's the one you wanna be wit'?" she said, placing raw chicken wings in a plastic bag and then shaking them in the seasoned flour.

I was blushing beyond my control. "I know that I love him, but sometimes I'm not sure if I exactly know how to love him," I said, pouring cooking grease into the black iron pot.

"What part are you not sure about?"

"Everything. Love itself."

"What's wrong with love?"

"It has too many sides, and as soon as you think you're on one side, turns out that you really on the flip side."

"So, you think you on the flip side of love?" she said, dropping a chicken wing in the iron pot.

I sat down at the table and crossed my ankles. "Flip side of love. Flip side of the game. One of 'em."

"Why don't you just take love and run wit' it?"

"Because I keep having dreams about dead fiends, and I'm not sure if I have the ability to commit with crazy shit floating around in my mind."

"You gonna have to let some of that stuff rest, Vera."

"And why would I do that?"

"So that you get a chance to breathe. If he a good man, keep him. Love him. Give him all that you can. True love is hard to find. Don't miss out, baby. Don't miss out."

"I gotta go, Rowanda. I need to leave," I said, cutting her off and pushing my chair from underneath the table. I couldn't take this any longer. I was beginning to feel sick, and being in the next room where an overdosed ghost was found dead with a lion's claw gash in her head was haunting me.

Biggie and Dirty had slipped out of the apartment and were smoking weed on the fire escape. The scent floated into the apartment, and it didn't seem to faze Rowanda one bit.

"Long as that's all they smokin', I don't mind. It's when they doin' dope, crack, crank, or angel dust that I have a problem," she said, stepping away from the stove and peeping out the window. After she closed the curtains back, she looked at me, as if me telling her that I needed to leave had just registered.

"What's wrong, baby? What happened?" she asked.

"Nothing. I just need to get going."

"Wait, wait," she said, looking as if she were holding back tears. "Take some of this food, please." She wildly opened the refrigerator and took out a bowl of corn, rice, and red beans.

"Wait, let me heat it up in the li'l microwave we have here. This a li'l somethin' that Biggie bought when I came outta detox. Wait one minute. The chicken is almost done. Tear that brown paper bag for me, and let me sit this chicken in that plate. Let some of the grease drain off." Tears were softly flowing down her cheeks as she moved like a gentle hurricane, hustling food like a deck of cards.

By the time I made it to the door, I had a grocery bag filled with food. She assured me that she understood why I didn't want to stay. "Hell, I would leave if I could, but Biggie and Dirty, they need me. You got Cookie, you got Taj. I ain't shit in your life, but it's okay. I understand. I ain't your mother no how. I's a crackhead."

I walked as quickly as I could down the hall. I ran down the stairs, and when I reached my truck, I was out of breath. Once I was inside my X5, I could feel my throat swelling up. I opened the door and threw up in the street. Then I felt like I wanted to cry. I closed the door, started driving, and watched the reflection of the projects disappear in my rear view mirror.

***

"Vera!" Aunt Cookie called early in the morning and said, "I need to see you."

"Aunt Cookie, it's six o'clock in the morning. What's the problem?"

"Tomorrow is Boy's birthday, and I wanna give him a little small party."

"I'll be there, Aunt Cookie. I'll be there."

I wanted to roll over and die at the thought of having to get outta bed. For the past couple of days, I had been unable to move. I hadn't been in the shop in three days, and I hadn't eaten in four.

I told Taj before he left for his shift at the hospital that I had the flu, but he rolled his eyes and told me not to play him for a fool. All of his things were there now.

I hadn't spoken to Rowanda since the other day on Lincoln Street. I knew that Aunt Cookie gave her the number, but it was not like her to call. She usually would just wait and show up at the shop or on Aunt Cookie's stoop.

I wanted to tell Taj that my period was late, but I wasn't sure how he would react, so I called Shannon.

"Your period is what?" she screamed in my ear. "What about your birth control?"

"Don't say nothing to Lee or Angie, but I haven't been using any. I keep forgetting to take the damn pill the same time every day."

"Well, you may as well get out of denial, 'cause yo' ass will not be able to hide a baby. Hell, you only live with a doctor."

"I know, and I haven't told him, but I think he suspects something."

"Why do you say that?" she asked.

"Because I'm always sick. Plus, the other day when I was gettin' my freak on, he put his fingers inside me, something he rarely does, because he usually uses his tongue—"

"A little too much information," Shannon said, cutting me off.

"Anyway, when he put his fingers inside me, it felt weird, like he was pressing on my cervix or something. I had to tell him to stop because the shit was hurting."

"So, let me get this straight. You were trying to bust a nut, and your man was doing a pelvic exam, peeping your whole card? And you think you got game? Girl, that nigga got you beat. Just tell his ass the truth."

"But I don't know how I feel about this."

"About what? I know you're not thinking about an abortion. We're getting too old for that shit. Look, tell the man. Let the man be happy. Get fat and pregnant, and let Lee and Angie get jealous because I'm the godmother. Fuck it. We only live once."

"Well, damn, I guess you have it all figured out."

"No, not quite, but I do know when it's time to stop playing games, and if you got a man that you love and want to be with, then do the right thing."

"You're right. I'm going out to buy the test now. Just to confirm it."

After I hung up, I went to the CVS down the street and purchased the pregnancy test. When I came back home, I sat down on the couch and tore open the pack.

Just as I was going into the bathroom to piss on the stick, the doorbell rang. I looked out the peephole and saw Shannon, Lee, and Angie.

What the hell? I thought. *What did they do, fly over here?*

"May I help y'all?" I said, standing in the doorway.

"You pregnant, ho?" Angie said. "And you told Shannon that she was going to be the godmother. Just fuck me, huh?"

"Yeah," Lee said.

"Fuck us, right?"

"I never told Shannon that."

"Yeah, right," Angie said. "I bet you didn't. Y'all some sneaky bitches! Every time I turn around, y'all got a buncha fuckin' secrets. This shit is being brought to end right here, though. Now, did you tell this ho that she was going to be the godmother?"

"First of all," I said to the three of them, "you're standing on my front stoop, telling my neighbors all of my goddamn business. Second of all, I never said nothing about Shannon being the godmother. And thirdly, I don't even know if I'm pregnant."

"Shannon," Angie said, tight-lipped, "I thought you said the nigga did a pelvic exam."

"Damn, you talk too much," Shannon said to Angie, pushing me to the side so that she could come through the front door.

"Would you go and take the test?" Shannon said, rolling her eyes at Angie.

I took a deep breath and went into the bathroom. I wasn't sure how to feel, because I never thought about having a baby, at least until now. Every other time I was pregnant, I knew what I was going to do, but now, I was not so sure. I did know that Taj would never go for an abortion.

Damn, what the fuck? Aunt Cookie would lose her mind when she heard this, but wait a minute: I may not even be pregnant. It could have been stress that had my period missing in action.

Goddamn, who was I trying to fool? I hadn't seen my period in almost eight weeks. And what made it so bad was that I had been fuckin' all the time. Every chance I got, I was droppin' hot coochie moves like a fuckin' Luke dancer. I should've known that this was bound to happen. I stood over the toilet and started peeing over the stick. Too afraid to look, I closed my eyes and imagined that there would only be one line instead of two.

After I finished peeing, Shannon knocked on the door and said, "Did you just get finished peeing? Hurry up and tell us what the stick says."

"You standing there listening to me pee? Y'all need a fuckin' life!"

I set the stick on the counter, cleaned myself, pulled up my pants, and flushed the toilet. I closed my eyes and then I eased them open so that I could look at the stick. I started with one eye open and left the other closed. I looked at it with the left eye first, and when I saw two lines, I swore that the left eye was wrong. I switched eyes, only to see the same thing.

Fuck! I picked up the stick and snatched the bathroom door open. Angie fell first, and then Shannon and Lee came tumbling behind her.

"It's positive," I said, fighting back tears.

"What's wrong?" Shannon said, dusting herself off.

"I'm having a baby."

"That's no reason to cry, Vera," Shannon said.

"Yes, it is," Angie insisted.

Shannon shot her ass a look and said, "No, it's not."

"Why are you crying?" Lee asked.

"Because," I said with tears falling and my words sounding muffled, "suppose I don't know how to be a good mother and my baby feels the same way about me that I feel about Rowanda?"

Shannon held me close and said, "We have already talked about this. You have to stop it. This is your baby. You will decide what type of mother you want to be. This is Vera's turn. Rowanda had hers."

"Do you want to have the baby?" Angie asked.

"Damn real she wants to have the baby," Lee said. "Right, Shannon?"

"Excuse me, but I'm the one pregnant. And yes, I will be having my baby."

"Good," Shannon said. "Now, Vera, I want you to get it together right now. You want to be a good mother, then start by not stressing yourself out. Do the right thing."

The girls stayed for over an hour and tried to make me feel better, but nothing worked. I was scared as hell. How was I going to raise a child if I'd been grown all my life?

Taj worked a double shift, so he didn't come home that night at all. Instead, he called and told me to meet him at Uncle Boy's party.

Aretha Franklin's new tune was blasting out the windows and into the street as I parked my X5. Taj had beaten me there, as I noticed his black Escalade seemed to take up half the block.

"Do you have to go back to the hospital?" I asked him, feeling like I wanted to throw up.

"Why? Do you need to go?"

"No, I don't think so."

"Just sit down and don't move."

Aunt Cookie strutted her stuff as she walked passed me smelling like violets. She wore a pair of white polyester bellbottoms, Payless platforms, and a black shirt with a white stitched collar.

"What it is! What it is!" she said, carrying a tray of Remy Red and dollar store flute glasses. "Show me whatcha workin' wit'!" she said to everybody in the room.

"That's my Cookie!" Uncle Boy said, already drunk and smelling like old rum. "Come on over here and gimme some o' that chocolate chip!"

Aunt Cookie's couch squeaked as I sat on it and tried hard not to move. The plastic on the cushions stuck to my skin and made it impossible for me to be able to sit in the same spot for long. I got up to go to the bathroom, and Aunt Cookie said, "Don't go too far, Babygirl"

I was trying desperately to tolerate her perfume, but it was only a matter of time before my tolerance would give out. "What's the problem, Aunt Cookie?"

"I dreamed up fried butter fish and rainbow trout."

"What?"

"You heard me. I dreamed up fried fish. Big, pretty fried fish."

"And your point?"

"My point? Oh, you being smart? Just watch yourself. Don't be around here gettin' pregnant. If you gonna be having babies, then make sure the nigga marry you, and I mean that. Don't be giving all the milk away."

She really needed to mind her business, considering she'd been living with Uncle Boy damn near all my life, but I wouldn't dare tell her how I felt about her concerns.

She left me standing near the bathroom door and headed toward Uncle Boy. That's when I noticed that Rowanda had just come in the house. Taj kissed her on the cheek. She seemed a little out of place, but I could tell she was pretending to be okay.

"Hey, Vee," she said, with droopy eyes, seemingly fighting off a nod. "How you?"

"Fine."

"Good. Good. Yo' mama fine too." She kept tooting her lips up, as if she were fighting off an itch, and making strange gestures with her face.

"Are you high?" I asked.

"What?"

"You heard me. Are you high?"

"Vee, I told you that I'm clean."

"You're lying!" I snapped. "I can spot a fiend a thousand miles away, and yo' ass is high!"

"What you care for?"

"Quite frankly, I don't give a fuck, but the least you could have done was got your hit after you left here."

"Vee, just go 'head and leave me alone."

"Don't tell me what to do! You ain't nothin' but a damn crackhead! I can't stand you!"

"You can't stand me? Tell me somethin' I don't know."

"What is goin' on over here?" Taj asked, squinting his eyes.

"Don't be looking at me like that! This trick is high!"

"Quiet down, Vera. This is not your show. Save that shit!" he said, waving his hands.

"Save what? That she's high? I knew she couldn't stay clean. Aunt Cookie was the only one fooled!"

"What is wrong wit' y'all niggas?" Aunt Cookie said, slightly drunk but trying to maintain her composure. "It's Boy's birthday. Be nice for once!"

"I'm leaving!"

"Vera, you better calm yo' ass down before Aunt Cookie step to yo' ass," Aunt Cookie said. "This your Uncle Boy's birthday, and as far as he's concerned, he only got one child, and that's you. So, you leave his birthday party mad if you want to, and watch how me and you fall out! Humph, you know how I do it!" She walked away.

"Get away from me," I said, tight-lipped, to Rowanda. "I can't stand your crackhead ass!"

"You can't stand me? You can't stand me?" she said, standing in my personal space. Her breath was stale as she spoke. "Let me tell you one motherfuckin' thing. I am your mother! You ain't had me! And another thing, I ain't one of your girlfriends, so you will respect me! Point blank, period.

"And no, I ain't never been the best mother, but I tried. I was fifteen years old when I had you, and soon as my mother brought you home from the trash dump, I knew that it was s'pose to be me and you.

"Now, I'm a little tired of the way you been treatin' me. And, by the way, I'm not a crackhead. I'm a dopefiend. Stop gettin' the shit confused. One thing's for sure, my dope is there for me, and it gets me to stop hearing you scream 'bout how much you hate me. I can get mama's blood offa me. I can get rid of Towanda's troubles, and I can leave Larry and his Coupe Deville on the corner, pimpin' me! To hell with you!" She stormed out the front door.

I went to say something to Aunt Cookie, but she just stared at me and said, "Don't say nothin', Babygirl. Don't open your mouth. You have done enough talkin' for the night!"

Step Twelve

When we came home, Taj didn't want to talk about Rowanda.

"We have other things we need to discuss," he said.

"Like what?"

"Like, when are you going to tell me that you're pregnant?"

"What?"

"Vera, don't start. Come with it. Now, when is my baby due?"

"How do you know I'm having a baby?"

"Vera, I'm a doctor and I live with you. You haven't had a period in close to two months. Your breasts are swollen, your nipples are dark, plus, when you were trying to get a nut, I slipped your ass a pelvic exam."

"Oh, so now you've taken it upon yourself to be my OB/GYN?"

"Stop playin' me, Vera. When is my baby due?"

"I don't know when the baby is due."

"Why not?"

"I haven't gone to the doctor. I just took the pregnancy test today."

"Well, make the appointment so we can go to the doctor."

"We? So, it's official?" I asked.

"What's official?"

"This?"

"What's *this*?"

"This baby and us."

He smiled and softly pushed his head into the plushness of my chubby abdomen and said, "Li'l man, tell your mother it's official."

The Platform

The word on the street was that Rowanda died. A dopefiend named Queen said that she got a hold of some bad shit and passed out in the two-dollar side of the abandoned building. Queen said that she spent her dope money to get to my shop, money that she got from suckin' dick. And she said she would spend it on Rowanda again if she had to, 'cause Rowanda meant too much to her to just let her go out like that.

"Yo' mama has been there for me. We lived on the streets together. We went to rehab together, relapsed together, shot up together, and we even did time together. Wasn't no way I was just gonna watch her die. I called the cops 'fo I left. I couldn't stay. I got a warrant for solicitation."

When I got there, I walked up the stairs of the boarded up house that was well occupied. People were on the porch and hanging out the windows. The breeze was filled with the scent of weed, the grass was spotted in-between dirt patches, and there were no trees. People of all shapes and sizes lined the porch and filled the hallways.

A li'l girl who was seemingly a woman sang a song into the tip of the crack pipe that her man snatched out her hand as he slapped the shit out of her for taking too long. The pregnant girl and the HIV chick shared the tip of a needle as they floated on cloud nine of a dopefiend's high. And, in the midst of it all, nobody gave a fuck. Everybody had their own set of issues, and the bitch laying across the kitchen floor passed out because she chose the wrong bag of dope was nobody's problem but her own.

"I thought you called the police!" I said to Queen.

"Nine-one-one is a joke. Ain't you heard? The po-po don't show up over here. You can call 'em, but they ain't gonna come. They figure it's just another nigga."

I wanted to let Rowanda die and remove myself of all the memories of her. I thought about how a dopefiend's funeral would be and what the pastor would say. Would he call my name in the eulogy? Would he think that she had it hard because of me? Would he say that Grandma was a testimony of strength because she raised three children with no daddy, all the while skin-poppin' dope? Would the pastor know that none of Grandma's kids made it past the seventh grade? Would he know that Rowanda was a dopefiend before she got her first period, and when she did get her period, it came nine months after she slept with a forty-year-old man who called himself Larry Turner? Larry Turner, who had a thing for little girls. Would the pastor talk about that? Or would he simply say, "God bless the child that has his own."

I let her hang on my shoulder as I guided her limp body down the stairs. Her legs hit each step like wooden pegs, and I could hear her breathing in my ear.

"Come on, Rowanda," is what Queen kept saying, sounding desperate, as if the time that she wasted catching the train from the Bronx to lower Manhattan would count for nothing.

"Come on, Rowanda!" Queen repeated, her voice elevating with every syllable. "Come on. Shit! What the fuck you tryin' to shut the light out for? What the fuck you tryin' to do!"

Queen's voice was like a drum beat, and Rowanda's breathing was like scratches in a rap song, and the dragging of Rowanda down the stairs, outside on the porch, and into my car was like a systematic rhythm that went "ba-boom, ba-boom, aahhhh." All I could think of was Sarah Vaughn, Dizzy Gillespie, and Billie Holiday. All I could hear was a jazz tune, a blues note. I could think of nothing else, nothing.

When we arrived at the hospital, the nurse seemed to have no respect for a used-up dope-fiend.

"Name?"

"Rowanda Wright."

"Spell it."

"What?"

"Spell it."

"Are you fuckin' crazy?" I screamed at the silly-ass triage nurse that kept tapping the tip of her ballpoint pen against the metal top her makeshift desk. "She is fuckin' dying and you asking me to spell her goddamn name!"

"Address?"

"I'ma slap the shit outta you if you keep askin' me these stupid fuckin' questions instead of getting her to a goddamn doctor!"

"And when she's done," Queen added, "I'ma stomp on yo' ass. You ever been stomped?"

"Security!" the triage nurse called. "Security!"

The security guard took his time strolling over to where we were. Apparently he was used to this nurse being threatened with ass kickings. He simply said, "Y'all gonna have to leave if you keep talkin' shit. Y'all gonna have to go."

"Fuck you!" Queen shouted. "Fuck you! This ain't no everyday dopefiend. This my damn friend. Ain't nobody seen my life like she seen my life. Don't nobody know. Don't nobody know!"

"Calm down," Taj said, standing behind me, breathing on my neck.

My shoulders relaxed, although I was surprised. Taj? I couldn't remember if this was the hospital he talked about this morning or not.

"Nurse," he said, sounding soft but firm, "please admit this patient to the E.R. immediately. All the other information can be collected at another time."

"What are you doing here?" I said to him.

"I work here on the weekends now, or did you forget? This situation with Rowanda, we need to deal with this. This is no good for the baby, this is no good for you, and it's starting to take over our life. But right now, your mother needs you. You should go inside so that you can be with her."

"My mother? That chick is not my mother!"

"What?"

"I'm not staying here to be by this bitch's side! Fuck her! What she ever do for me but put me in a trash dump and hide out on the corner 'til the garbage man heard me cry? I gotta go!"

"You keep on runnin'!" Queen shouted at me, while I was going through the hospital's round-about. "You keep on runnin'! She don't need you. She got me! She ain't no everyday dopefiend. She my friend, goddamnit! My friend! Fuck you!"

Taj watched me rev my X5 out of the parking lot and haul ass. *Fuck them*, I thought. I didn't need not even one of them. Not Taj, not Queen, and damn sure not Rowanda.

By the time I tipped in the door to check on Aunt Cookie, the house seemed asleep. All the lights were out, and the only thing shining was the small wicker lamp that she kept on the end table. She usually left Marvin Gaye playing softly on the CD player, as she made her way up the stairs to sleep.

"Marvin was my nigga," she used to say when I was little. "That was my man, and the day his daddy shot 'im straight fucked Cookie Turner up.

As I walked toward my old room, I heard the crushing of the orange speckled industrial carpet that Aunt Cookie got on sale at fourteen cents a square yard in 1972. She refused to change it, because she said that she hadn't gotten her money's worth out the shit, and the man she bought it from said that it was due to last a lifetime. She also kept the plastic on her red crushed velvet living room set, because she said that people were always touching her shit, and she didn't want them messing up her "bad-ass furniture" that she regarded as a classic.

The stream of the light from the wicker lamp reflected off the windowpane and led a valley of blue down the dark hallway.

Peeking in Aunt Cookie's room, I saw Uncle Boy's feet hanging off the side of their queen-sized bed. Aunt Cookie was sitting in the dark, staring out the window, with a silk scarf tied around her head, smoking a cigarette.

"Aunt Cookie, what you still doin' up?"

"Waiting to see what time you was gonna come tippin' in here."

"How did you know I was coming here?"

"'Cause of what you did. How you showed yo' ass at that hospital. How you was up there cussin' like a mu'fuckin' fool."

"How did you know that?"

"Taj."

"I ain't have to be there! Queen came to get me. I didn't have to go. I could have let her die!"

"You could have let her die? You got some nerve playing God, Vera!"

"To hell wit' Rowanda! What she ever do for me?"

"What she ever do for you? Every goddamn hustle she ever had was because of you! She ain't have to take care of you for the little time she had you. She could've let you die, but she didn't, and when she lost you, she still fought for you. The day they took you, she walked all the way from Lincoln Street to my house. She said she saw you bangin' on the car windows hollering and screaming, but she kept walking, because she needed to do something, something to save you."

"Really? That's interesting. I guess that in between her sessions of sniffin' dope, she placed me in a trash dump. That's sure to get her Mother of the Year."

"Say another word and I'ma slap the shit outta you! Now, you shut the hell up and listen, and you listen good! Rowanda ain't never had nothing from the start. All she ever known was them drugs. Ain't no life like the one for a dopefiend.

"She came and she got me. She told me 'bout you, and I ain't wait. I came for you, and this the bitterness that you show my love. This is it?"

I just stood there. Tears rolled down my cheeks.

"You keep goin', Vera, and you keep killin' yo'self 'cause you hatin' yo' mama. Keep it up and you gonna die long before she does. You better wake up, 'cause everybody has got a story, Vera. Everybody."

All night, I lay in the bed and fought off memories of dopefiends. The crack pipe played in my mind like an eight track, or a scratched-up record with a stuck needle. I could hear lingering clinks of silver belt buckles across porcelain sinks as I made my way outta the bed and to the face of the toilet.

I stared at the water going around and around as I flushed the routine evening sickness of my stomach down the drain. The circles of water raced through my mind, and each time I heard the faucet drip, I would jump. I refused to move and let anybody in, because nobody knew what it was like to have lived all your life feeling like a newborn in a trash dump.

The phone was ringing, and I refused to pick it up.

"Nothing is that bad, Vera," Lee and Angie said on the answering machine. "Nothing."

"I'ma just let myself in if you don't answer the phone," Shannon insisted.

I didn't hear Taj when he came in. Seeing my hand on the side of the toilet, barely hanging on, he broke down and almost cried.

I slipped to the floor, weak and disoriented, wondering why I could never get over the heartache inside. Taj lay on floor, and there we were, face-to-face, with our cheeks resting on the cold porcelain, laying it all on the line.

"I always thought that I could live without Rowanda. I always thought I could be me by myself, but she never allowed me."

Taj just listened.

"I love my Aunt Cookie, let me just say that, but she's not my mother. My mother is some crackhead dopefiend that has me trying to kick her drug habit.

"There are so many people I have seen in my life who didn't care about me. I had to learn to survive, and hustling men is what got me through, not knowing that it was that same hustle that would bring me full circle with myself.

"Until I met you, I didn't know what it was like to be in love, or how to truly love someone in love with you. I didn't know how to treat them, because I didn't know how I wanted to be treated. So, I used men and I played them, thinking that it would make up for me feeling like a crying newborn in a trash dump.

"I feel like all my life I've been pretending that all fifty-two cards in my deck are aces. Shit, life is a mu'fucka."

"Life is mu'fucka? Life is a mu'fucka?" he said, raising his head from the base of the toilet. "What is wrong with you? You been living your life out a dressed-up trash dump? So, what you're telling me is that Cookie, Boy, Lee, Angie, and Shannon don't mean shit just 'cause Rowanda is crackhead?

"You got to love you, Vera. Vera has to be Vera's best friend before Vera can make love, give love, or be about love. You think you're the only child who's ever been given birth to but never had a mother? You think you're the only one that has ever cried!

"Get yo' ass up off this floor and get it together! What are we doing at the neck of the shit bowl?

Get up! And don't you drop not one more pitiful tear! Life ain't a mu'fucka. Life is what you make it!

"Come on, baby," he said, holding me. "I know you're stronger than this. Go see your mother."

I spent three hours riding around the hospital parking lot, trying to figure out what to say and what to do. At first, I thought about going to see if she died, but then I thought about what would happen if I couldn't tell her how I felt. What would happen if I couldn't tell her that I still felt like a newborn in a trash dump? What would happen if I couldn't tell her that I used to dream of her coming home and being clean, of her coming to get me? What would I do if she died? Would I die?

Her eyes were closed when I first entered the room. I stood over her for what felt like hours, but when I checked my watch, only five minutes had past. Her body seemed frail, and she had tubes coming from everywhere.

"Okay, I'm here," I said to nobody in particular, and nobody in particular answered. The room was dark, and the only light that came drifting in was from the nurse's station. Flashes of red and blue filtered throughout the room.

I stood in one spot and looked around. I puckered my lips and bit the inside of my jaw.

"You know, Rowanda," I said to her as she lay there, showing few signs of life. "Life is a mu'fucka, and that's the God's honest truth." I felt my throat welling up, but I couldn't cry now. I had something to say.

"You've always been my shadow. Everywhere I went, everything I did, there you were. I could never be released from you, and how I prayed that you would die. How I prayed that you would overdose and die. But when the opportunity came, I carried you on my back and tried to save you.

"You have given me the strength and determination that I have today to be nothing like you. I don't know who you are or what you are. All I know is that you are my mother, and I've never had a mother before. And you know why? Because nobody will let you die! So, I tell you what, don't fuckin' die on me now! Don't fuckin' go. I need you. I need to hear your story."

I lay my head down and pushed my face on the side of her hip and deep into the white sheet. I could almost taste the smell of her skin.

I thought that I was dreaming when I woke up with crust on the side of my mouth and Rowanda's hand stroking my hair.

"I'm sorry, Vera," she said in a whisper. "I'm sorry I ain't never been no good. All my life I ain't been shit."

I went to say something, but she asked that I just listen.

"Larry Turner was my mother's man, but he loved me. He was the only one that showed me what it was like to be loved and cared for, so I betrayed my mama and I stayed with him. My mother took you 'cause she said you was the child she was s'pose to have with Larry.

"All I have ever known is dope, and when crack hit the scene, I was a full-fledged fiend. I ain't never been shit!"

"Rowanda," I said, cutting her off.

"No, you let me talk. All my life, I have had my mother sell me to men, sell me to women, sell me to whoever would give her money for dope. When I was hungry, Mama was shootin' up the food. When I was down, Mama was high, and when I needed love, I thought I had Larry Turner by my side, but he didn't care either. And when I told him I was pregnant, he laughed. He laughed and told me I was a bitch, a used-up bitch who wanted his money.

"I never wanted his money, I just wanted to be loved. My mama used to say, 'That's what you get, bitch! That's what you get!'

"The only people that ever treated me like somebody was Towanda's boys, Cookie, and Queen. Ain't nobody else, including my own child, ever gave a fuck about me. And so, I needed something to get me away. Something that made me feel like I could do anything I wanted to do. The dope needle was dick for me, you understand? The dope dealer was my man, and whatever I needed to do to keep him, I did, no matter what the cost. If I ever crossed over and went to the other side, then that would be a price that I had to pay."

"So, what you saying is that you gonna punk out and die on us now?"

"Us?"

"Yes, us. I'm having a baby, and I need you. We need you."

"Humph," she said, sounding exhausted. "Am I gonna punk out and die? Hell, no! All your life, I been dead. Now I wanna show my grandbaby what it's like for me to be alive!"

The End